HERMAN J. VIOLA

······

NORTH AMERICAN INDIANS

ILLUSTRATIONS BY BRYN BARNARD

CROWN PUBLISHERS, INC., NEW YORK

Published by Crown Publishers, Inc., a Random House company, 201 East 50th Street, New York, New York 10022

CROWN is a trademark of Crown Publishers, Inc.

Map art by Eleanor Hoyt

http://www.randomhouse.com/

Library of Congress Cataloging-in-Publication Data
Viola, Herman J.
North American Indians / by Herman J. Viola ; illustrations by Bryn Barnard. — 1st ed.
p. cm.
Includes bibliographical references and index.
Summary: 1. Describes the lifestyles of various Native American groups
before the arrival of the Europeans.
1. Indians of North America—Social life and customs—Juvenile literature.
2. Indians of North America—History—Juvenile literature.
[1. Indians of North America.] I. Barnard, Bryn, ill. II. Title.
E98.S7V56   1996
970.004'97—dc20   96-8179

ISBN 0-517-59017-4 (trade)
0-517-59018-2 (lib. bdg.)

Printed in the United States of America

10 9 8 7 6 5 4 3 2 1

First Edition

Photographic credits follow the index

CONTENTS

NORTH AMERICAN CULTURE AREAS

THE ARCTIC

AN ATHAPASKAN
SKIN WIGWAM
Chapter 7

AN INUIT ICE
IGLOO
Chapter 8

THE SUBARCTIC

A HAIDA
PLANKHOUSE
Chapter 5

THE
NORTHWEST

THE GREAT
PLAINS

AN IROQUOIS
LONGHOUSE
Chapter 4

CALIFORNIA
AND THE WEST

THE
NORTHEAST

A SIOUX TIPI
Chapter 6

A ZUNI PUEBLO
Chapter 2

A CHUMASH
THATCHED
HOUSE
Chapter 3

A CHEROKEE
CLAY HOUSE
Chapter 1

THE
SOUTHWEST

THE
SOUTHEAST

INTRODUCTION

WHEN CHRISTOPHER COLUMBUS reached the Americas in 1492, he found people no one in Europe had met before. Thinking he had reached the Indies, he called these people Indians. The name has stayed with them ever since.

Although our knowledge of the native peoples of North America at the time of Columbus is incomplete, certain facts are clear. For example, we know that relatively few Indians lived in what is today Canada and the United States compared to the numbers that lived in Mexico, Central America, and South America. Perhaps two million people were living in the United States and Canada. In the rest of the Americas, the number may have been as high as thirty-eight million.

Of the two million Indians in North America at the time of Columbus, more lived along coastal waters than in the interior of the continent. More lived on the Pacific coast than on the Atlantic coast. More lived in the South than in the North.

Despite their small numbers, the Indian peoples of North America were very diverse. It is incorrect to speak about *the* American Indians because they are not one people. In terms of language, appearance, and way of life, the native peoples of North America were as dissimilar from each other as were the peoples of Europe. Some Indians lived in wooden houses. Some lived in skin houses. Some made wooden boats. Some made boats of bark or skin. Some used dogs to carry or pull their belongings. Some ate dog meat. Others would only eat it in times of starvation. Some Indians were warlike. Others thought war was barbaric.

Differences like these are considered "cultural." When anthropologists, the scientists who study people, use the word "culture," they are referring to the entire way of life of a people. Different Indian tribes that lived near each other, shared a similar way of life, and spoke a similar language are said to share the same "culture" and are grouped together in a "culture area."

In this book we will look closely at eight culture areas and the distinctive lifestyles of the Indians who lived in them. It provides a glimpse of American Indian life at the time of first contact with Europeans. This moment differed from tribe to tribe and region to region. The Indians of the Caribbean met Columbus in 1492. The Florida Indians met their first Europeans less than twenty years later. The Polar Inuit did not meet their first Europeans until 1818, more than three hundred years after Columbus arrived. Some tribes, especially those living along the Atlantic coast, were completely destroyed as a result of the initial contact because of diseases such as smallpox, measles, and influenza, which they contracted from the Europeans they met. Other tribes in the interior of the continent, such as the Indians of the northern Great Plains, at first enjoyed a "golden age," resulting from material goods such as metal tools, cloth, beads, guns, and horses they obtained from Europeans. A few groups, such as the pueblo Indians of the Southwest, retain a certain amount of their original homeland and traditional culture to this day.

The book also features essays written by members of different tribes. The reason for this is to show that Indians are as much a part of American life today as they were five hundred years ago. They have gained distinction in the classroom and the courtroom, on the playing field and the battlefield, in government, the arts, and all aspects of modern American culture. They have enriched the heritage and history of all Americans.

1

THE SOUTHEAST:
A CHEROKEE VILLAGE

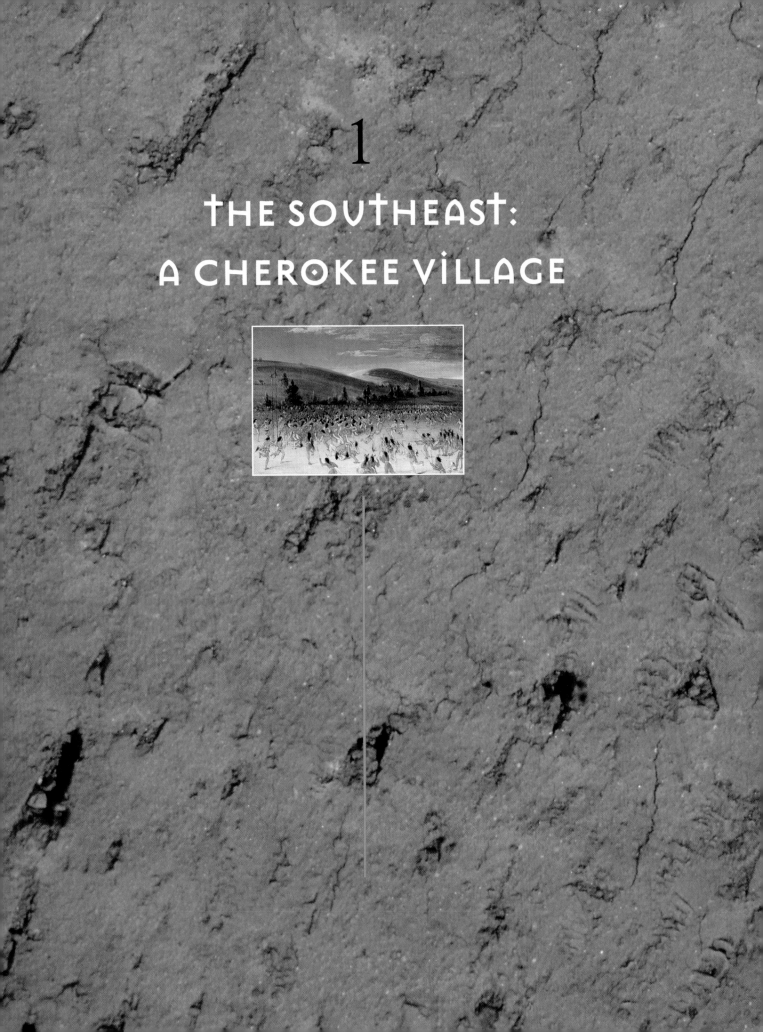

In this village scene from the Southeast, two Cherokee women are using wooden pestles to grind corn in a mortar made from the hollowed-out stump of a tree. The cutaway view of the summer house shows a Cherokee family: a mother tending to her baby, a little boy, and a father setting out with his blowgun, seeking a bird or squirrel for the evening dinner. Cherokee houses were neatly

painted with whitewash made from ground oyster shells. On the eaves are squash, pumpkin, and ears of corn from the village garden. In the background is the village's large ceremonial and council house, built on a raised earth mound.

THE SOUTHEAST REGION AND SOME SELECTED TRIBES

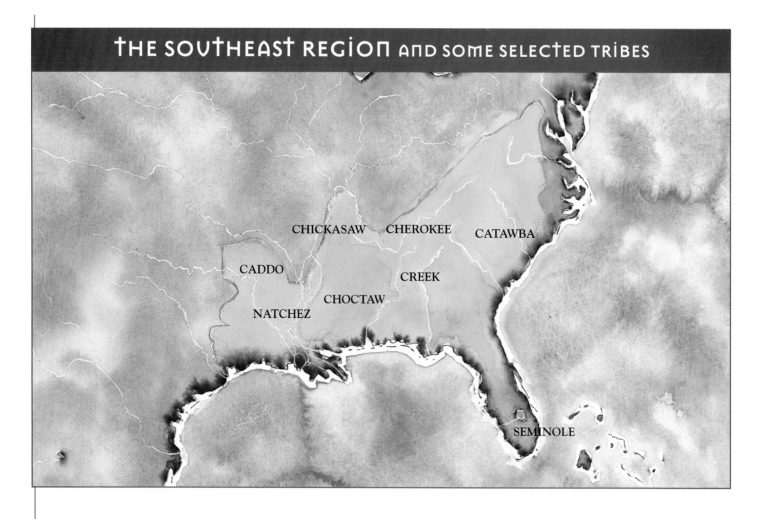

THE SOUTHEAST IS a broad region of coastal plains, saltwater marshes, pine barren forests, and rugged hills and plateaus that stretches across the southern part of the present-day United States from Texas to the Atlantic Ocean. Its climate is characterized by mild winters, warm summers, and abundant rainfall. In times before Columbus the region was rich in wildlife, as well as nuts, fruits, and edible plants.

More than two dozen Indian tribes lived in the Southeast at the time of Columbus. They belonged to what is called the Mississippian culture, but little is known of these peoples because their way of life was so thoroughly disrupted by the first Europeans who visited them. Among the first of these was the Spanish explorer Hernando De Soto. During the four years that his army traveled through the Southeast, from 1539 to 1543, his men destroyed many villages and killed hundreds of Indians. Thousands more died of diseases left in his wake.

With the decline of the Mississippian culture, other tribes began to dominate the Southeast. They spoke two distinct languages, the Muskogean and the Iroquoian. The Muskogean speakers include the Creek, Choctaw, Chickasaw, and Seminole. The Iroquoian speakers include the Cherokee.

MOUNDVILLE: A Mississippian Town

THE INDIANS encountered by Hernando De Soto in the sixteenth century belonged to what is called the Mississippian culture, which flourished in the southeastern United States for several hundred years before the time of Columbus. These Indians lived in large cities and built earthen mounds that looked like flat pyramids. On top of the mounds were temples and houses for rulers and religious leaders. Mississippian society was very structured: nobles, commoners, and slaves answered to one leader, who had the powers of a king.

Moundville was a Mississippian town located on the banks of the Black Warrior River in present-day

Alabama. At its peak between A.D. 1200 and 1500, it covered hundreds of acres of land and included at least twenty mounds. In this picture, a noble's house stands on a mound in the background; many others like it were built on mounds around the edge of the town. In the center was a plaza and a great mound on which stood a temple.

Inhabitants grew corn—shown here being carried in baskets—and other crops such as beans and squash in the fertile soil along the river. They hunted deer and other game, and trapped fish in enclosures in the river called weirs. Log canoes, shown here pulled up to the riverbank, were used for fishing and transportation.

Although these tribes were not as structured and well organized as the Mississippian peoples, they were like them in many ways. They formed powerful confederacies—leagues in which several tribes joined together to defend and support each other. They raised foods such as corn, beans, and squash. They had cities, temples, and strong governments.

The Cherokee lived in the southern Appalachian Mountains. Because there were so many mountain ridges and valleys in their homeland, the Cherokee had divided into four bands that lived so separately that it was not always easy for them to understand one another, even though they had originally spoken the same language.

A Cherokee legend explains why their homeland had so many hills and valleys. According to this legend, water once covered the earth. When the water finally drained away, the land was too wet and swampy for anyone to walk on it. The animals, therefore, kept asking the birds to fly over the earth and let them know when it was dry. One of the birds that helped the animals was Grandfather Turkey Vulture. He was a giant bird with great wings. By the time he got to the land intended for the Cherokee, however, he had become so tired his wing tips were brushing the ground. When his wings flapped down, they dug valleys; when they flapped up, they created mountains. The animals, who were watching him from their seats

on a rainbow, called him back before he had made hills and valleys over the whole earth. It was too late for the Cherokee, however, and that is why their homeland was so mountainous.

Like most of the other Indians in the Southeast, the Cherokee built two kinds of houses. Winter houses were round and made of earth. Summer houses were made of large posts stuck into the ground, with smaller posts placed between them. Then the Cherokee wove willows and other branches between the posts, much like weaving a basket. They covered the wicker-like walls inside and out with clay, which was then painted white using a solution made from powdered oyster shells.

These summer houses could be very large—about 16 feet wide and up to 60 feet long, although most were shorter. One family lived in each summer house. There were usually three rooms—one each for cooking, eating, and sleeping. Sometimes there was a covered porch along one side. The fire was in the middle of the floor, but there were no chimneys; smoke just went out through the thatched roof. Beds were on platforms along the inside walls.

In each Cherokee village there was a large ceremonial and council house, where

▶ *This beautiful carved wooden figure was probably made by the Cherokee's neighbors, the Caddo. Its hair and mustache are made from human hair, and between its knees it clutches a cloth bundle. Its purpose, whether ceremonial or decorative, is not known.*

meetings were held. The villages were governed by a council of elders, but anyone could attend the meetings.

Like most of the eastern tribes, the Cherokee were farmers. A family usually had two gardens and tending them was the responsibility of the women. One garden was close to the house and the other was in a communal, or shared, field some distance away. Corn was a very important part of the Cherokee's diet and they planted at least two types. One ripened so quickly that they could plant two crops in one season. This type was planted in the family garden near the house and was boiled or roasted as it ripened. The other type of corn was left out in the communal field to dry before harvesting. This corn was then stored and used for making hominy.

Hominy is boiled corn, a lot like the "grits" that some Americans eat today. It was made by placing corn kernels, water, and wood ashes in a pot and letting them soak overnight. The water was then drained and the kernels were placed in a mortar, a kind of bowl made from the hollowed-out trunk of a tree. Cherokee women then used a wooden pestle, which looked like a baseball bat, to pound the corn kernels and break the hulls. After throwing away the hulls, the women then pounded the corn into a fine flour and used it to make corn bread, which was a favorite Cherokee food.

The pots used for cooking were made by Cherokee women and girls from clay. The women first shaped the pots and then, after drying them in the sun, placed them in the middle of the hot ashes left over from a large fire. If this was done properly, the finished pots would be as hard as glass and have no cracks.

Cherokee women were also expert basket makers. Baskets were woven from strips of river cane. By using cane of different colors, the weavers could make baskets with intricate and beautiful designs.

▲ A decorated clay pot made by the Cherokee's neighbors, the Catawba.

▼ This cane basket, also from the Catawba tribe, is typical of the baskets used throughout the Southeast region.

Although there were many different kinds of fish in the lakes and rivers of Cherokee country, not everyone would eat them. Some thought fish brought bad luck. The Cherokee much preferred to eat meat, especially that of the whitetail deer. Cherokee men also hunted bears, opossums, rabbits, and squirrels. For hunting, they used bows and arrows and blowguns—long, hollow tubes of cane through which darts could be blown.

Blowguns were very accurate weapons.

Each Cherokee belonged to one of the seven Cherokee clans. Four of the clans were called wolf, deer, bird, and paint. The remaining three have Cherokee names for which there is no English translation. A Cherokee away from home could always find food and shelter in the home of a clan member. Cherokee inherited their clans from their mothers, and women owned all the land in Cherokee families. When a

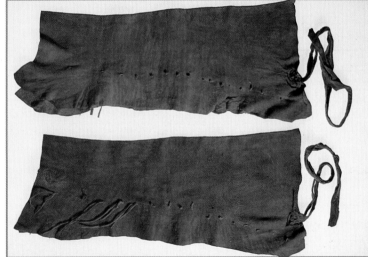

▲ A pair of men's leggings made from deerskin by the Seminole Indians of Florida.

◀ A Cherokee hunter using a blowgun made from a hollow cane. Cherokee blowguns could be as long as 12 feet and could kill small animals such as squirrels and rabbits up to 100 feet away. Darts were made from the hard wood of the locust tree and tipped with thistles.

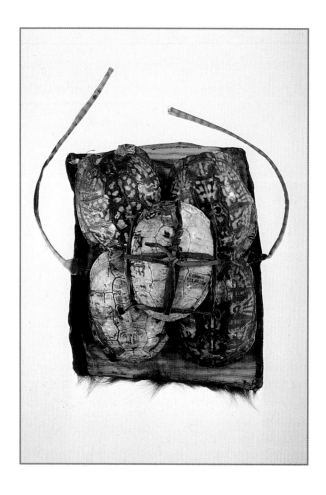

A Cherokee turtle-shell leg rattle. Women dancers wore rattles like this tied around their ankles during ceremonies such as the Green Corn Ceremony. By carefully controlling their movements, skillful dancers could make the rattle sound only at the right moments.

Cherokee man married, he went to live with his wife's family, but he did not become a member of her clan.

Clans had many important functions. One was to resolve disputes. For example, when a Cherokee killed another Cherokee, the victim's clan members could seek revenge by killing the murderer. If the murderer ran away, then one of his close relatives, such as an uncle or a brother, could be killed in his place. Sometimes relatives even volunteered to die in place of the real killer. Relatives could also give valuable things to the victim's clan as a way to settle the blood debt. Once this was done, there was no further disagreement between the clans.

Cherokee life involved many ceremonies, such as the Green Corn Ceremony, a four-day feast that celebrated the fall harvest. These ceremonies always featured singing and dancing. The Cherokee made several musical instruments. One was a water drum, made from

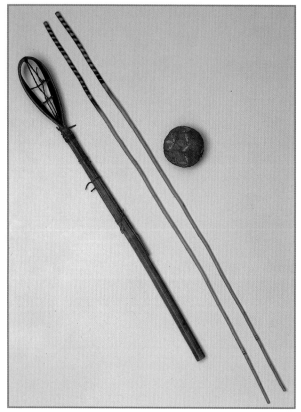

Sticks and ball used for playing the ball game.

The ball game. This picture, painted in 1834 by George Catlin, shows a game in progress between two Choctaw towns. The goal is on the left. In front of the goal, a crowd of players fights for the ball.

the hollowed-out trunk of a log. The drum was partly filled with water. By varying the height of the water, the player could change the tone of the drum. The Cherokee also made rattles out of gourds and turtle shells.

The most exciting ceremony was the ball game. This game is the ancestor of the modern game of lacrosse. The Cherokee called it "the little brother of war" because it required the same skills that warriors needed when going into battle: strength, endurance, quickness.

The game was played on a grassy area larger than a modern football field. The opponents were two equal teams from different Cherokee towns, and there could be as many as a hundred players on each team. Each player carried two sticks about three feet long with little nets at the end. The ball was made of buckskin stuffed with deer hair.

The object of the game was to score a goal by throwing the ball between two tall posts about a foot apart at opposite ends of the field. The first team to score twelve goals won. Players could pick up the ball using only their sticks, but they could throw it with their hands. There were few rules, so games were very rough and many players received bruises and broken bones. The competing towns would bet valuable things on the games, which could last anywhere from a few minutes to many hours.

In the 1830s, the U.S. government forced the Cherokee to leave their homelands and settle in Oklahoma (see sidebar). However, a small group of about 1,500 Cherokee escaped relocation and hid in the mountains of North Carolina, where their descendants still live.

Today the Cherokee's tribal headquarters is in Tahlequah, Oklahoma. They are the most numerous Indian tribe in the United States, with more than 200,000 people claiming Cherokee blood.

THE TRAIL OF TEARS

THE CHEROKEE WERE among the first Indian groups to meet Europeans, and they readily adopted white ways. By the early 1800s the tribe had its own written language, devised by George Guess—better known as Sequoyah. The tribe had its own constitution, a Cherokee-language newspaper, tax-supported schools, well-tended farms, and large cotton plantations.

However, whites in the Southeast wanted the land belonging to the Cherokee and other tribes for themselves. Under pressure from whites, Congress agreed to move the Indians. In 1830 it passed the Indian Removal Act, forcing the removal of all eastern Indians to lands across the Mississippi River. Besides the Cherokee, these included the Choctaw, Creek, Chickasaw, Seminole, the Sac and Fox, and the Miami.

The tribes appealed to the courts for protection and in 1832 won their case in the U.S. Supreme Court. However, the government and the army ignored the court's ruling and began forcing the Indians to leave. Between 1830 and 1839 the tribes of the Southeast were forced to leave their homelands, culminating in 1838-39, when the Cherokee were marched west to Oklahoma. Disease and lack of food and proper clothing caused great suffering: more than 4,000 Cherokee died during the 800-mile trek. The Cherokee still call the path they took the "trail where they cried," or the Trail of Tears.

MIXED HERITAGE BY ANNIE TEAMER

My daughter and I have just returned home from spending the day at a powwow. She is eight years old and very excited over having danced in her Indian clothing for the first time. She worked many hours in her Indian Education Class preparing for this day. I watched her dancing from a distance, noticing how beautiful and proud she looked. Her excitement had lasted throughout the day, and all the way home she has been talkative and full of questions.

Now we are finishing dinner and sitting around talking at the kitchen table. This is a perfect time to talk about our heritage. I explained that we have multiple heritages—Native American, African American, and Jewish. Our family has always acknowledged our Jewish heritage, our African heritage is strong, and we are working to keep our Indian heritage just as strong. Most of the Indian people we know are of mixed heritage. My daughter interrupts me to name the mixed heritages of some of them: Puerto Rican/Cherokee/Arab; African American/Navajo; Mohawk/Italian; Sioux/Filipino. All of these people are also very proud of their heritages.

My early childhood was spent in Tennessee with my grandmother, who was Blackfoot/Cherokee. She was a proud, beautiful, and wise woman who was very respected in the community and extremely knowledgeable in the use of herbs—so much so that people would consult her when they were ill. She was also a wonderful storyteller with a great sense of humor. Most of her stories were about animals. Grandmother did a lot of sewing and was an excellent quilt maker. I still have a very special quilt she made for me in my teens. Now that Grandmother is in the spirit world, I know that I can never again get anything like the beautiful cherished things she made for me.

When I was of school age, I was sent to live with my parents in the Midwest. I loved school and enjoyed studying about Native Americans in my history class. I would occasionally raise my hand to answer questions or to tell the class that I was part Indian. I noticed that some of the students were excited about the fact and some seemed a bit puzzled. I suspect the puzzled students had the Hollywood stereotype in mind: high cheekbones, red skin, long black hair. Maybe they would have been convinced if I had worn feathers, buckskin, and beads. However, throughout my years in school, I also noticed that more and more students were identifying themselves as having Native American heritage. I further noticed that a large percentage of those students had a heritage similar to my own. It seemed that more and more people were becoming educated about the existence of Indian people of mixed heritages.

When I worked for the Title IV Indian Education Program, it was always a pleasure talking to parents, students, and teachers. I wanted to do my part in teaching about Native American heritage and culture. It is important for people to know that we come in different sizes, shapes, and colors and that Native Americans, like other ethnic groups, intermarry and have done so for hundreds of years.

So tonight I tell my daughter how proud it made me feel to see her out there dancing and carrying on our tradition. I tell her to always stay close to the Indian community and to try to educate others about Native American culture. I tell her to have patience with people who make insensitive remarks about Indian people of mixed heritage; that it is out of ignorance that they do so. I tell her the importance of showing respect to everyone, especially the elders, and for her to always keep a strong sense of identity, culture, and pride in all of our heritages.

Annie Teamer is of Cherokee, Jewish, and African heritage. She lives in New York City, where she works as the coordinator for volunteers at the National Museum of the American Indian–Smithsonian Institution. Previously she was a home/school coordinator for the Title IV Indian Education Program.

2

THE SOUTHWEST:
A ZUNI PUEBLO

The Zuni lived in large apartment houses made of a sun-dried mixture of mud and straw called adobe. The walls were made of adobe bricks and were neatly whitewashed. The roofs were also made from adobe, supported with large logs. The walls had windows, but no doors: families entered their apartments by climbing ladders through entrances in the ceiling. The roofs of the

pueblos were at once streets, playgrounds, and work areas. On the roofs in this picture are large ovens that look like beehives, where the Zuni baked bread made of cornmeal. A young woman is carrying a pot filled with water to her apartment, while in the background a woman making pottery and several men at work adding a new room to the pueblo can be seen.

THE SOUTHWEST REGION AND SOME SELECTED TRIBES

HOPI

MOHAVE NAVAJO

YUMA ZUNI

APACHE

PIMA

THE SOUTHWEST IS a vast and varied region of rugged mountains, lush river valleys, endless prairies, and interminable deserts. It includes all or part of the present-day states of Arizona, New Mexico, Colorado, Utah, Nevada, and Texas, as well as northern Mexico. At the time of Columbus, it was home to dozens of Indian tribes that differed as much from one another as did the land they lived upon.

At least three different lifestyles could be found among the Indians of the Southwest. Some tribes, like the Navajo and Apache, were fierce hunter-raiders.

Other tribes were peaceful farmers and hunter-gatherers, like the little-known Mohave and Yuma Indians who lived along the lower Colorado River in what is now southern Arizona.

The third group are the pueblo Indians, who are famous for their large, multi-roomed dwellings that resemble the apartment houses of today. Built of stone, wood, and dried earth called adobe, pueblo houses had as many as five floors and a hundred or more rooms. Sometimes an entire town of a thousand people lived in a single large apartment house.

THE NAVAJO

NEIGHBORS TO THE pueblo Indians, the Navajo were a warlike people who fought their more peaceful neighbors and later the Spanish and the Americans. From the Spanish, the Navajo acquired sheep, and they became experts at raising them and weaving woolen clothes and blankets. Sheep raising is still an important part of Navajo life and Navajo blankets are sold for high prices. The Navajo are also famous for their silver and turquoise jewelry.

The Navajo moved at different times of the year to find grass and water for their livestock. Their principal dwellings were called hogans—log and mud structures that looked a little like wooden igloos and blended into the landscape. A blanket-covered doorway faced east, and there were no windows. The circular shape symbolized the sun. The logs were laid on top of each other, gradually meeting at the center to form a dome-shaped roof. Dirt was then piled on the roof and tamped down. In the center of the roof was a smoke hole about three feet square.

Hogans had no furniture. The family slept on sheepskins on the floor. Belongings were kept in baskets hung from roof beams or tucked into crevices between the inside logs. Navajo families often had several hogans in different places for use at different times of the year.

Because of constant warfare with the Spanish, who tried to enslave them, the Navajo took refuge in the mountains of Arizona. There they defended themselves until they were defeated in 1863 by an American army led by Kit Carson, and forced onto a reservation far away from their mountain homeland. The Navajo call their removal "the long walk."

The Navajo were permitted to return to their homeland in 1868. Since that time, they have been friends of the United States. During World War II, some 3,000 Navajo joined the U.S. armed forces. Some became known as the Navajo Code Talkers. They sent messages over the radio using a secret code from their own language. The code was never broken by the enemy.

Today there are more than 200,000 Navajo, most living on a 16-million-acre reservation that covers parts of Arizona, New Mexico, Colorado, and Utah. The tribal name comes from a pueblo word meaning "the people with large fields"—although the Navajo themselves prefer to be called Dine, which means "the people."

A hexagonal (six-sided) Navajo hogan built of logs with an earth-covered roof. Hogans could also be cone-shaped or square and completely covered in earth. The word hogan means "homeplace."

A Navajo woman's shoulder blanket.

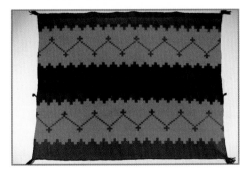

Contrary to what many people believe, the word *pueblo* is not the name of a tribe. It is a Spanish word that means "village" or "town." When the first Spanish explorers met the Indians who lived in these complex houses, they called them "pueblos" to distinguish them from nomadic Indians like the Navajo and Apache, who never stayed very long in one place.

Pueblo buildings were like great forts. The bottom floor usually had no windows or doors. To enter their houses, families used a ladder or a pole made from a tree trunk with steps carved in it. They climbed onto the roof and then entered their rooms through a hole in the roof. When greeting guests, pueblo families would say: "Please climb up and climb down." At nighttime, or if enemies appeared, the ladders would be pulled up and the people inside would be safe.

A typical pueblo family lived in a room about 12 feet by 14 feet. The adobe walls would be neatly white-washed. In the corner would be a chimney and fireplace large enough to hold logs three feet long. The room would be rather dark except for the light from the fire or from the hole in the ceiling. A

stone or adobe bench around two walls would be used for sitting or as a shelf. Niches in the walls served as cupboards. Clothes hung from deer antlers or wooden pegs. Cooking was done in pots made of clay. Drinking water was kept in gourds, which also made good drinking cups.

Pueblo peoples liked to eat a kind of bread made from cornmeal and stews made of meat, chili

peppers, and corn. Because corn was such an important part of the pueblo diet, girls had to spend three or four hours each day grinding it. On the floor along one wall of a room there would be three narrow bins made of stone slabs for grinding the dried corn kernels into powder. Each slab was of a different texture: very rough, not so rough, and very fine. Behind each slab was enough space for a girl or woman to kneel facing the room so she could talk and visit as she worked.

When it was time to eat, most pueblo family members took the blankets they were wearing and folded them up to sit upon. At night they slept in a row using the same blankets and perhaps a couple of robes made of rabbit skins.

The pueblo Indians made and wore clothes of cotton cloth. Unlike most of the other Indians who lived in North America, pueblo peoples were growing, spinning, weaving, and dyeing cotton before they met Europeans. They used tanned deerskins to make moccasins and the yucca plant to make sandals. They were also skilled potters and jewelers.

Even though we call all these "apartment-living" Indians pueblos, they actually belonged to several separate groups or tribes. The various pueblo peoples spoke different languages, and differed in other ways as well. The decorations on their pottery and baskets differed from village to village, as did certain costumes and ceremonies. Nonetheless, there were also many similarities. Their houses, their

◄ *Hopi girls grinding corn. The butterfly hairstyle was traditional for unmarried women. Once married, women wore their hair in a braid.*

▼ *Zuni eating utensils. On the left, an earthenware bowl decorated with geometric designs, and on the right, a ceramic ladle and spoons. The small spoon in the center is decorated with a bird figure.*

crafts, and their lifestyles were very much alike and they all were farmers who lived primarily on corn, squash, and other foods that they planted in their gardens.

The Zuni, who today live about 40 miles southwest of Gallup, New Mexico, were representative of the pueblo peoples. Like most of the other pueblo peoples, the Zuni were descended from a prehistoric people known as the Anasazi, who built huge stone villages throughout much of the Southwest more than a thousand years ago.

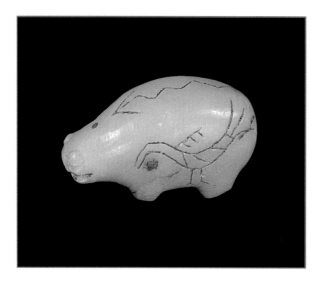

▲ A tiny Zuni stone carving of a bear. Small animal carvings like this one, called fetishes, were believed to bring protection or good fortune to their owners.

Although the ground was hard and dry much of the year, the Zuni were very successful farmers. Zuni farmers grew at least six different kinds of corn, including some that were colored blue, black, and red, as well as yellow and white. The Zuni farmer planted corn by using a special stick to punch holes through the hard topsoil. He made the holes about six feet apart and into each one he placed about twenty kernels of corn. Throughout the growing season, he carefully tended his cornfield. He carried water to his plants and protected them from birds and animals until it was time to harvest the ripe corn. This would be in the fall after the first frost.

Although the men did most of the work in the cornfields, the crop was considered the property of all the women in a Zuni household. The first ears of corn from each crop were welcomed into the house with a special ceremony. "My children," the Zuni mother would say, speaking to the corn, "how have you been these many days?" The other women in the house, speaking for the corn, would reply: "Happily, happily."

After the corn was harvested, it would be spread on the roofs to dry. The Zuni, like their pueblo neighbors, would usually try to keep a year's supply of corn in storage as protection against a crop failure. If the harvest had been a good one, Zuni roofs would almost groan from the weight of the stacks of corn that filled every available space. The best ears would be saved to use as seeds for the following year.

Although the pueblo Indians ate many different kinds of plants, as well as a variety of nuts and fruits, they also liked to eat meat once in a while. Sometimes the men and boys would hunt deer and antelope. These were hard to catch using bows and arrows, so they would try to drive them into traps or over cliffs.

Jackrabbits were much easier to hunt. In fact, hunting rabbits was as much fun as going on a picnic for the pueblo peoples. Both men and women would form a large circle and try to drive the rabbits into the center of it. The men carried special clubs that looked like boomerangs, which they would throw at the jackrabbits as they tried to run away. When a rabbit fell over, the girls would race ahead and try to get it. The man who hit the rabbit gave it to the girl who brought it to him. The girl, in turn, would have to give him a nice meal the next day. This was a way boys and girls sometimes met the person they would marry.

The Zuni had a highly structured society. Each person belonged to a clan inherited from the mother. A clan would be made up of one or more families related on the mother's side, and it was forbidden to marry someone who was a member of one's own clan. After getting married, a man went to live with his wife's family. The Zuni were a theocracy, which means the heads of the Zuni religious groups gov-

▼ Hopi bow and arrows and boomerang-like rabbit stick.

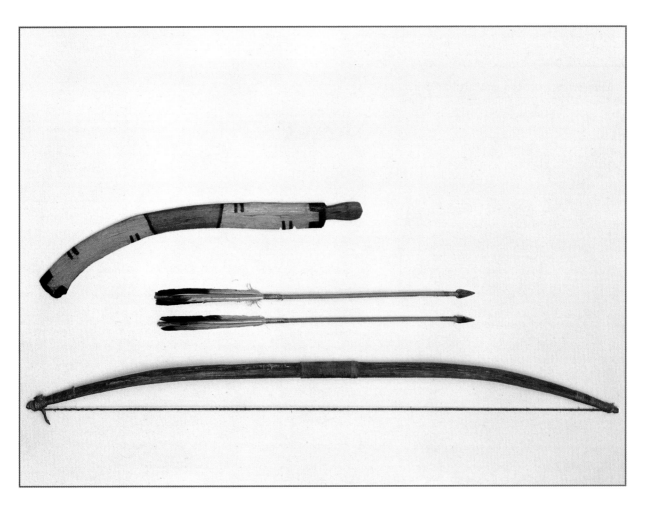

erned the people through a council. These religious groups also directed the dances and other ceremonies that took place in the pueblo. All Zuni males belonged to a "kachina" society into which they were initiated as young boys. The kachinas performed their religious rites in six "kivas," which are like churches. Each kiva represents one of six directions: north, south, east, and west, and "above" and "below." Members of the different kachina societies wore special costumes that represented spirits associated with Zuni religious life.

◆

The Zuni, like the other pueblo peoples,

are independent and strong-willed. They have retained much of their culture and language to this day, despite considerable pressure to change—first from the Spanish (see page 32), then from Americans from the East. Today pueblo Indians live in pueblo towns and villages in New Mexico and Arizona that are in many ways similar to those they lived in five hundred years ago, before the arrival of the conquistadors, or Spanish conquerors.

▶ *A Hopi kachina doll.*

▼ *A Hopi painting shows a ceremonial dance, led by a member of a kachina society wearing a special kachina costume.*

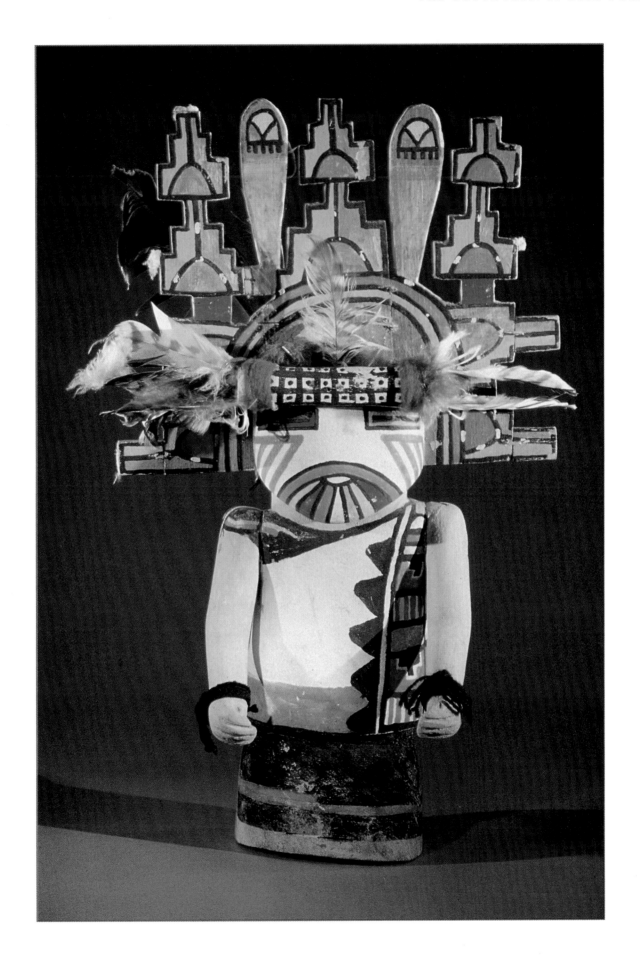

THE CONQUISTADORS

THE FIRST EUROPEANS to reach the Southwest were the Spanish "conquistadors," or conquerors. Conquistadors liked to compare themselves to medieval knights—but most were ruthless men who placed personal wealth above all other values. The famous Hernán Cortés, the Spanish explorer who conquered the Aztecs of Mexico, once declared: "My men and I suffer from a disease that only gold can cure!"

The first of the conquistadors to enter the Southwest was Francisco Vásquez de Coronado, who came seeking imaginary "cities of gold." He arrived in 1540 with almost three hundred soldiers. The Zuni people tried to resist Coronado, but their stones and arrows were useless against the Spaniards' armor and guns. Coronado stormed the pueblo and looted its food supplies before continuing on his way. Coronado reached as far north as central Kansas before abandoning his search and returning to Mexico City.

In 1598 the Spanish returned under the leadership of Juan de Onate. The pueblo people at first welcomed Onate. They gave him and his followers food and shelter and allowed his priests to preach and to baptize converts to Christianity. The

This picture, dating from 1791, is thought to be one of the first images of warfare between the Spanish and the Indians. Armed only with bows and arrows, California Indians confront a Spanish soldier on horseback.

Spanish soon wore out their welcome, however. Spanish soldiers began to treat the Indians brutally, and Indian labor was exploited on Spanish farms and ranches. The Indians' traditional religious practices were outlawed. In 1680, under the direction of a religious leader by the name of Pope, the pueblo Indians united and drove the Spanish out of the Southwest and back to Mexico.

When the Spanish returned to the Southwest fifteen years later, they behaved differently. For the next two hundred years, until Americans from the East began arriving in the Southwest, the Spanish and the pueblo Indians lived together in relative peace.

But elsewhere in the West the oppressive treatment of Indians continued. In California, where Spanish priests and soldiers began building missions in the late eighteenth century, war between the Indians and the Spanish continued until Spanish rule in North America ended in 1821 (see Chapter 3). The relatively peaceful coexistence of the Spanish and the Indians in the Southwest meant that the pueblo culture survived Spanish rule, while the California Indian culture entered a decline from which it would never recover.

THE WORDS BY LORIS ANN MINKLER

I shifted in my seat on the hard stool for the umpteenth time. Beads of sweat burned my eyes as I strained to see over the shoulders of the women sitting in front of me. Then someone behind me said, "They're coming." The tingling of bells in the distance grew louder with the pounding excitement in my chest.

The familiar steps of soft moccasin against hard earth made small puffs of dry earth fly. The kachinas entered the plaza, laden with a bounty of harvest and gifts for everyone. The crowd hummed with anticipation. It was the after-lunch dance. The bowls of fruit placed on the floor of the plaza caught my eye. They were full of apples, oranges, cherries, strawberries, peaches, and colored eggs. I wondered which one would be mine.

The kachinas began their first song. Mother turned to me and said, "Listen to the words." The words! Why did Mother have to spoil the fun? The words were always serious uncle talks. Sometimes the words were hard. Sometimes they were soft. When Mother or Father spoke the words, it often meant that I needed a special remembering. Sometimes I had a lot of rememberings. Sometimes the words left my head because my memory didn't work. Sometimes I was bored by the words. And sometimes I didn't hear the words. That's when Mother would tell me I needed a new pair of ears.

The first song was almost finished. I couldn't wait to get my bowl of fruit. I stood up to get a closer look. The kachinas seemed larger, wavering gently in the heat wave. Their song grew louder and louder, filling the air until it reached all the way to the sun. Then right before my eyes, each word of the song transformed into soft light with wings. The words, like magical butterflies, touched the faces of little children and caressed the wrinkles of every grandma and grandpa. The words floated from one person to the next until everyone in the plaza was connected. It was like one giant halo.

● ● ●

"Give her room. Give her water." Mother's voice came from a distance. I squinted. Faces hovered close to mine, spilling hot breath into my hair. It was difficult to breathe.

"What happened?" I asked.

"You had a heat stroke," Mother answered.

I lurched myself upright. The kachinas were gone. The bowl of fruit was also gone. Tears welled in my eyes. "Was I bad?" I asked. "I tried to remember the words, Mama.

"Treat people with respect. Pray for all living things. Share. Behave. Be kind to everyone. Work hard. Don't be lazy. Get up early each morning. Love yourself. Pray for rain, long life, and good health. The kachinas are watching. The kachinas are watching."

The words tumbled from my mouth and I mumbled them over and over again. The kachinas must have known that I did not pay attention to the words. I was a bad girl. Tears made a path down my cheeks. For once, I was not ashamed to cry.

"Look what the kachinas left for you." Mother was beaming. In her hand was the prettiest pottery I ever saw. The bowl was heaped to the top with bananas, grapes, eggs, oranges, and lots and lots of cherries. My favorite.

"The kachinas called your name. But by then you had already fainted." Mother handed the bowl of fruit to me. "By the way," she said, "rain sprinkled on us all during the last song. There was only one small cloud in the sky."

My heart leaped with joy. Our prayers had been heard. It was a very special day.

Tomorrow, I will be ninety years old. I can still hear the song as clear as the hot summer day when I was only eight years old. Every time the kachinas come, I see the giant halo through my blurred vision, blessing the entire village. The words belong to my grandchildren now.

Loris Minkler lives in the village of Oraibi on the Hopi Reservation in northeastern Arizona, considered to be the oldest continuously inhabited community in North America. She is Associate Director of the Hopi Foundation and in 1995 was a delegate to the Fourth World Conference on Women in Beijing, China.

3

THE WEST:
A CHUMASH THATCHED HOUSE

This picture shows a Chumash family at their home overlooking the California seacoast. The women in the foreground are
grinding acorns into flour that they will use for making mush or cakes. Inside the house a woman is making a basket, while in the
distance along the shore several Chumash canoes are being readied for a fishing trip. The Chumash built their house out of tule

reeds, cattails, ferns, and sea grass. The thick walls kept the families cool in summer and warm in winter. Tule mats hanging from the roof were used as walls to make separate living spaces for the members of a Chumash family.

CALIFORNIA AND THE WEST AND SOME SELECTED TRIBES

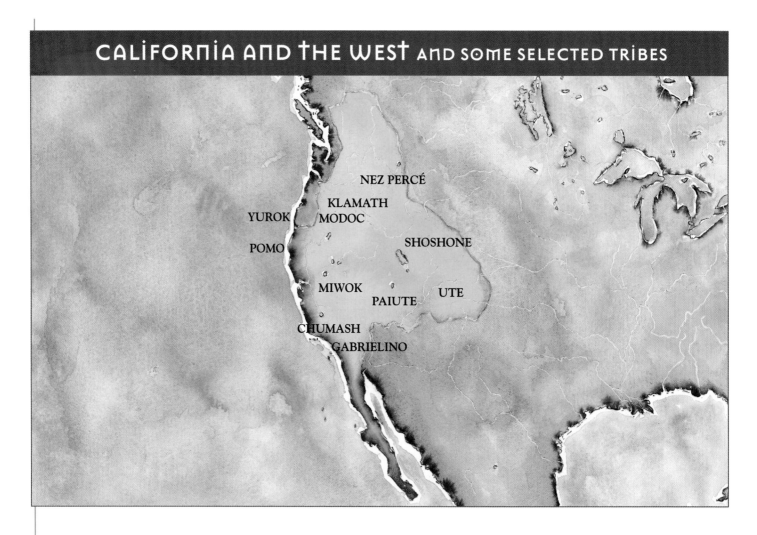

THE CALIFORNIA REGION occupied an area about two-thirds the size of the modern state of California. Although it was small in size, the region was densely populated and featured a broad range of environments—valleys, foothills, mountains, seacoast, and desert. The California Indians were primarily hunters and gatherers who depended upon the particular kinds of foods that could be found in the areas where they lived. In northern California, the primary food of the Indians was salmon. In central California it was acorns. In southern California it was acorns, wild seeds, fish, and small animals.

Only in southern California did any of the Indians grow their own food.

California Indians depended upon the foods nature provided, and they treated nature with respect. They did not pollute the rivers lest the salmon refuse to return each year. When collecting acorns, they took care not to break the branches of the oak trees. In their yearly harvests, they did not take more than they needed so there would be enough food when they returned the following year.

At the time of Columbus, as many as one hundred different tribes and bands lived in California—more than in any

Flails, like this one made by the Pomo tribe, were used by California Indian women to knock seeds into collecting baskets.

other area of North America. These groups were as varied as the California landscape. They differed in language, in physical appearance, and in the way they lived.

Although California was densely populated, most of the tribes in it were very small, often no more than large bands. One exception were the Chumash (pronounced "CHOO-mahsh"), who were much more numerous and structured than many California Indian groups. The Chumash lived along the California coast north of present-day Los Angeles. Their territory

NATIVE AMERICAN LANGUAGES

AT THE TIME of Columbus, it is estimated that more than 2,000 different languages and dialects were spoken in the Americas. The total number spoken in North America was about 550. At least 200 are still in use today.

There was only one region of North America where everybody spoke the same language. That was the Arctic. The language of the Inuit peoples had only two dialects. Inuit living from Siberia to Greenland—a distance of over 3,500 miles—could understand one another.

Frequently, even tribes living very close to one another spoke different languages. In California, for example, were to be found about one-third of all the Indian languages spoken in what is today the United States and Canada. Even different bands belonging to the same tribe might speak very different dialects. The languages spoken by the various Pomo bands were similar in origin, but when spoken

they could differ from one another as much as French and English do. This means that individuals from widely separated Pomo bands often could not understand each other.

In other areas of America, neighboring tribes spoke the same language. The Dakota, or Sioux, for example, spoke the Siouan language. The Mandan, Oto, Winnebago, and several other tribes living on the Great Plains and in nearby areas also spoke Siouan.

The number of Indian languages still being spoken dwindles with each passing decade. This is a matter of grave concern to many North American Indians because their native languages are a vital part of keeping their culture, history, and religious traditions alive. Many Indian tribes now teach their children their own language in school along with English and other languages.

was vast—as much as 7,000 square miles in extent. It included high mountains, lush valleys, and seacoast as well as the four large islands off the California coast now known as the Santa Barbara archipelago.

The Chumash lived year-round in thatched houses made of tule (a reed that grows in marshy areas), ferns, cattails, or sea grass. To Spanish explorers, who first met the Chumash in 1542, these houses looked like oranges cut in half.

Tule houses were easy to build and well suited to the climate of central and southern California. The thatched walls, which could be six inches thick, protected Chumash families from cold winter winds and kept them cool during the hottest days of summer. When the thatch got old and moldy or filled with insects, the Chumash family simply burned the house down and built a new one.

To make a thatched house, the builders first drew a large circle on the ground and then stuck willow poles in the ground every two feet or so around the circle. The tops of the poles were tied together, then the builders tied thin willow poles horizontally around the upright poles. Upon these the Chumash hung the folded reeds or grass used to make the thatched walls. To keep out mice and other rodents, the builders heaped dirt around the base of the house. The Chumash, like other native peoples of the Americas, liked to have the doors of their houses open either

to the east or to the west so as to face the rising or setting sun.

The Chumash divided the insides of their houses into rooms by hanging tule mats to make "walls." Tule mats were also used as mattresses. These rested on bed frames that were built as much as four or five feet off the floor. The floors were usually bare earth pounded down with rocks or logs to make them hard. Some Chumash families covered the dirt floor with clean white sand from the beach. In the center of the floor was a fire pit surrounded by flat rocks. Above the fire pit was a smoke hole.

For furniture, Chumash families made stools and tables out of wood or large bones from whales. Sections of the backbone of the whale made comfortable chairs.

The Chumash were skilled craftspeople. The women made beautiful and intricate baskets that were so finely woven they could hold water for a short time. To make the baskets permanently waterproof, the Chumash sealed the insides with asphaltum, a type of tar that seeped into ponds from oil deposits far below ground.

Chumash men were equally famous for their plank canoes. Plank canoes were about 25 feet long and made from many small wooden planks that were sewed together through drilled holes. Asphaltum was used to make the seams and holes waterproof. Chumash boatmen used

THE MISSIONS

DURING THE SEVENTEENTH and eighteenth centuries, Spanish Jesuit and Franciscan priests established dozens of missions in frontier regions of North America.

The missions were large plantations. Each one had fields for growing crops, pastures for cattle, sheep, and horses, and a village where Indians lived. The dominant structure was a large building with adobe walls. In it was a church, a kitchen, rooms for the Spanish priests, and guest rooms for visitors. A *presidio*, or fort, was sometimes attached to the mission. Spanish soldiers protected the priests and guarded the Spanish frontier against Spain's rivals in America, such as the French, the English, the Portuguese, and the Russians.

By the end of the eighteenth century, the missions formed a great arc across North America, from Florida and South Carolina in the east to Texas, New Mexico, Arizona, and California in the west. In California a chain of 21 missions linked San Diego and San Francisco along 600 miles of the Pacific coast.

Missions had several goals. They extended Spanish rule into North America, but they were also intended to "civilize" and convert Indians to Christianity—while using their labor for economic gain. Priests taught the Indians about Christianity and the Spanish way of life. Mission Indians grew wheat, grapes, and corn. They raised sheep, cows, and goats; cared for horses; and learned European methods of weaving, carpentry, and brickmaking.

Although missions were intended by their founders to do good, they often caused great harm. The Indians preferred their own religious customs and resented having Christianity forced upon them. Indian societies were forcibly uprooted and relocated. In California, in particular, large numbers of Indians died during the mission period, as a result of disease, starvation, and conflict with the Spanish.

Mission Indians repeatedly rebelled. The most successful uprising took place in 1680, when the pueblo Indians who lived near Santa Fe, New Mexico, killed as many as 500 Spaniards and chased the rest from their country. The mission system fell into decline after Mexico gained its independence from Spain in 1821. By the middle of the nineteenth century, when the United States extended its territory into New Mexico, Arizona, and California, the missions had become extinct.

This picture, painted in 1832 by Ferdinand Deppein, shows a small version of the kind of dome-shaped reed house built by the Chumash. In the background is the Spanish mission at San Gabriel.

canoes to travel to the islands off the California coast and to fish in the Santa Barbara channel. The Chumash and their neighbors the Gabrielino are the only North American Indians known to have plank canoes. The skill and ingenuity with which the canoes were built greatly impressed the Europeans who saw them.

Another important tribe were the Pomo (pronounced "PO-mo"), who lived in central California west of the Sierra Nevada mountains and north of present-day San Francisco. Like many other California Indians, the Pomo were not a structured tribe. They were groups of people who lived near each other and shared a similar lifestyle and language. At the time

▼ *A replica of a Chumash plank canoe, built in 1976 for the Santa Barbara Museum of Natural History.*

of Columbus there were thirty or so Pomo bands with populations ranging from about a hundred to perhaps as many as a thousand.

Each Pomo band occupied a small territory. This territory was seldom more than 20 miles wide. In each one would be a main village, where ceremonies were held, and perhaps one or two additional smaller villages. In their villages the Pomo, like the Chumash, built houses made of tule reeds. These reed houses could be very large. Some could hold several families. The biggest ones were used for ceremonies attended by forty or fifty people.

Because the Pomo needed to travel in order to find the foods they liked to eat, they also built a portable house made of large slabs of bark stripped from giant red-

wood trees. These houses could be quickly and easily built. Using tools made from the antlers of deer and elk, Pomo men would pry large sections of bark from the trees. These they leaned against one another to form what looked like a wooden tipi.

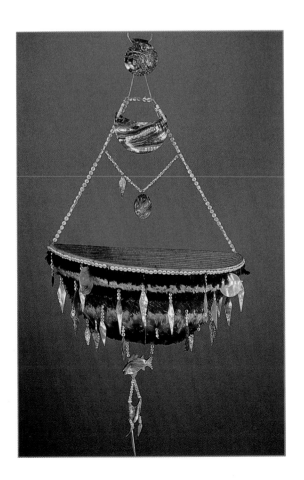

Four baskets, showing the great skill of California basket weavers.

◀ *Pomo basketwork tureen for feasts.*

▲ *Pomo funeral basket.*

◀ *"Sun basket," decorated with shells and feathers.*

▼ *Gift baskets decorated with feathers, clamshells, and abalone. The smaller of the two is a child's basket decorated with red woodpecker feathers. This basket was given to a child at the age of about seven, and it was believed that if it was lost or given away, the child would suffer great misfortune.*

Pomo men and women were short in stature, stocky, and strong. It was not unusual for a Pomo person to carry a loaded basket weighing 100 or more pounds many miles. The baskets, which were carried on their backs, were attached to their heads with a strap called a tumpline.

Pomo women were well known for their patience and powers of concentration as well as their strength. Patience and concentration were expressed in the beautiful and intricately designed baskets they wove from willow branches and other plants. Pomo baskets are considered some of the finest ever made in North America. Woven in many shapes and sizes, they were often decorated with colorful bird feathers, seashells, and beads.

Pomo women and children gathered most of the food for their families. Their staple food was the acorn, which they gathered in the fall from oak trees. These nuts were plentiful in the foothills where the Pomo lived, but preparing acorns so they could be eaten safely was a long and

▼ *A Pomo woman weaves a basket from willow branches. Behind her are tipi-like houses made of redwood planks.*

A PLATEAU TRIBE: THE NEZ PERCÉ

TO THE EAST of the coastal regions of present-day California were two less populous regions: the Great Basin and the Plateau. Much of the Great Basin was dry and harsh, and the Indians who lived there foraged for roots, seeds, berries, and other wild plants and hunted lizards, snakes, and other small animals. To the north, the Plateau region varied from rugged semi-desert to well-forested woods and mountains.

Because they were situated between the Great Plains to the east and the Pacific coast to the west, the Plateau peoples shared many traits with their neighbors in those areas, and they became noted traders. They exchanged buffalo robes and dried meat from the plains for dentalium shells, dried fish, and other goods from the Northwest coast. And when horses reached the Plateau country in the early 1700s, they became an important part of the lifestyles of several Plateau tribes.

One of these tribes was the Nez Percé. This name, given to them by French traders, means "pierced nose"—a mistake, since members of this tribe did not usually wear ornaments in their noses. The Nez Percé call themselves Nee-me-poo, which means "real people."

When horses became part of their culture, Nez Percé bands began making long trips out of the mountains eastward to the buffalo ranges in

A Nez Percé horse collar decorated with beads and bells.

Montana and Wyoming. These bands often stayed on the plains a year at a time, before returning to their mountain homeland laden with dried buffalo meat and decorated robes. The buffalo-hunting Nez Percé also began to live in hide tipis.

The Nez Percé homeland in the Plateau featured acres and acres of lush meadows and was an ideal environment for raising horses. Soon the Nez Percé had vast herds of excellent horses that were the envy of their neighbors. These horses became an important trade item.

When Lewis and Clark made their trek across the American continent in 1805, they met the Nez Percé and were fed and treated with great kindness. Unfortunately, they were followed by fur trappers, settlers—and diseases that carried away a third of the Nez Percé.

Many of those who remained were eventually persuaded or forced to sell their land and move to reservations. However, several bands refused. When the U.S. army tried to force them to move, they resisted, and in 1877 war broke out. Led by Chief Joseph and others, these bands tried to escape to Canada, where they hoped to continue their former way of life. Scores of Nez Percé died; a few escaped, but most, including Chief Joseph, were imprisoned or exiled in Oklahoma.

Today, about 2,000 Nez Percé live on a reservation in Idaho.

tedious process. First they had to be shelled, dried, and pounded into flour. Then the flour was spread in shallow, sandy basins and soaked in hot water to remove bitter-tasting tannic acid. The remaining mush was placed in water-filled baskets, and hot stones were dropped into the baskets to heat the water to make acorn meal. The meal could be eaten as gruel or wrapped in leaves and baked into cakes.

Besides acorns, the Pomo ate berries, seeds, and roots. From the sea came fish, kelp, barnacles, and mussels. From the land around them came animals such as deer, bear, and wood rats. The Pomo also loved to eat insects such as hornets, wasps, and grasshoppers, which were considered very tasty when cooked. To catch grasshoppers, the Pomo made a circle around a large grassy area and set it on fire. When the grass stopped burning, the grasshoppers trapped in the circle would be cooked and ready to eat.

Using tule reeds, Pomo made canoe-like boats, which they used for hunting, fishing, and collecting duck eggs. Because they were fragile, these boats were used only on quiet lakes and streams.

Pomo "shamans"—men and women who combined the skills of a priest and a doctor—could cure all sorts of illnesses through their knowledge of herbs and plants. Some shamans used a tube made from a bone to suck the disease or evil spirits causing a problem from a sick person's body.

◆

Few of the California Indians survived the arrival of Europeans and, later, white Americans in their homeland. Most of the many bands and tribes that lived in California disappeared during the nineteenth century as a result of diseases introduced by Europeans, warfare, and the forced removal from their homelands. Those who refused to leave their homelands were often killed by European invaders who did not appreciate the beauty and intelligence of their way of life.

Many of the Chumash, who were a very peaceful people, worked for the Spanish at their missions (see page 41). When the missions were closed in the mid-nineteenth century, many Chumash disappeared with them. Today several thousand Chumash and Pomo still live in California, although little remains of their original way of life.

A FISHING FAMILY BY LOUISE JEFFREDO-WARDEN

My grandfather was born in 1904—as was his father, in 1872—at an inland village site near Los Angeles that was once called Sibangna by the Native Americans who originally lived there. When the Spanish began arriving in southern California to found settlements three hundred years ago, they founded a mission at this place and renamed it San Gabriel Archangel. But Mission San Gabriel was not the original home of our people, nor was "Gabrielino"—the name given by the Spanish to the Native Americans they removed there as slaves—our traditional name.

For at least eight to nine thousand years, our people lived far west of Sibangna. Before Europeans and European-Americans invaded our homeland and virtually destroyed our populations and way of life, we were founding large towns and trading centers in southern California along the Los Angeles and Orange County coastlines and on the offshore islands of San Nicolas, Santa Catalina, and San Clemente. At some of these towns as many as 1,500 people lived year-round. We were called "westerners" and "islanders" by some of our neighbors, whose arts, religions, sciences, and technologies we greatly influenced.

My father used to tell me that in those days, being a fisherman was an extremely risky occupation. Like our neighbors the coastal Chumash, we built plank boats for fishing purposes. But our boat, called a *ti'at*, was designed to withstand heavier surfs and rougher seas. We also traveled much farther out on the open seas than did the Chumash. Many men lost their lives on voyages out to catch the larger fish like tuna, swordfish, sea bass, and shark. Special societies of expert, high-ranking men made such voyages. In much the same way as chiefs received their offices, these men received their knowledge and training about fishing, seafaring, and spiritual matters through select family lines.

As far back as I can remember about my life, and as far back as my father can remember about his, there was always talk of fishing in our family. There were stories about how my great-grandfather would pack his wagon with children and belongings and make the long trip from San Gabriel to the beach. Once there, he would camp and fish, teaching his children for weeks at a time. And when the state began charging my relatives for fishing licenses they could not afford, they moved their excursions still farther south, to the scorching beaches of northern Mexico. Though plenty of good food, like *apu*, or abalone, waited there, so did sharks menacing the shoreline and huge, aggressive rattlesnakes wriggling lickety-split across the sands!

Today it is generally believed that nothing remains of the island and coastal "Gabrielino" or their culture—that we are extinct. But my family's lineage worked against all odds to keep the cultural significance of fishing and seafaring alive for its children. Like his father before him, my grandfather was an extraordinary fisherman who knew the southern California waters like the back of his hand. Though his immediate family had not lived on the islands or at the coast for more than 150 years, my grandfather—a chemist by profession—held state and world records for surf fishing.

His friends and relatives say he fished with graceful, perfectly timed movements that were unequaled by others. Standing on the beach and watching him cast out so much farther than the other fishermen was, they say, like watching "poetry in motion." He also fished from boats on the open sea. Though he was only 5 feet 8 inches tall, he was a handsome and powerful man who could expertly tire out and reel in even the greatest of fishes.

My grandfather died when he was much too young and I was just a toddler. I did not have the chance to know him well, but I grew up surrounded by the sight of his accomplishments—his beautiful awards and trophies for all kinds of fishing. He was a sportsman of such renown that there were also plenty of newspaper articles about him, and wonderful still photos of him, for me to read and study. One of the most fitting comments I ever read about him was that he was "always teaching." Indeed, when I look at my grandfather's trophies, I think about our history and my heritage. In this way, my grandfather is still teaching. His trophies remind me—as they will remind my daughter—never to forget that ours is a fishing family.

A writer, folklorist, and award-winning poet of mixed European and Native American descent (Island Gabrielino/Pay̱omkawish [Luiseño]/Creek), Louise V. Jeffredo-Warden is a doctoral candidate at Stanford University. She is pictured here with a photo of her Island Gabrielino and French grandfather, John Edward Jeffredo. The photo was taken at a southern California beach in 1926. An enrolled member of the Temecula (Pechanga) band of Luiseños through her grandmother's lineage, Louise enjoys writing in both the Luiseño and English languages.

4

THE NORTHEAST:
AN IROQUOIS LONGHOUSE

In this Iroquois longhouse, a family is preparing an evening meal. Ears of corn hang from roof beams, where they are being dried to use as seeds in the next planting season. Along the right wall are the platforms that Iroquois families used for beds and seats. Above it is another platform, used as more sleeping space or as a shelf where the family can store clothes, dried foods, and other

necessary items. As many as twenty families could live in one longhouse. The only doors were at the ends, so people got to their "apartments" by walking down the center passageway. In the passageway are small fire pits, shared by the families living on either side. Smoke escapes through small openings in the roof that can be covered with bark when it rains.

THE NORTHEAST REGION AND SOME SELECTED TRIBES

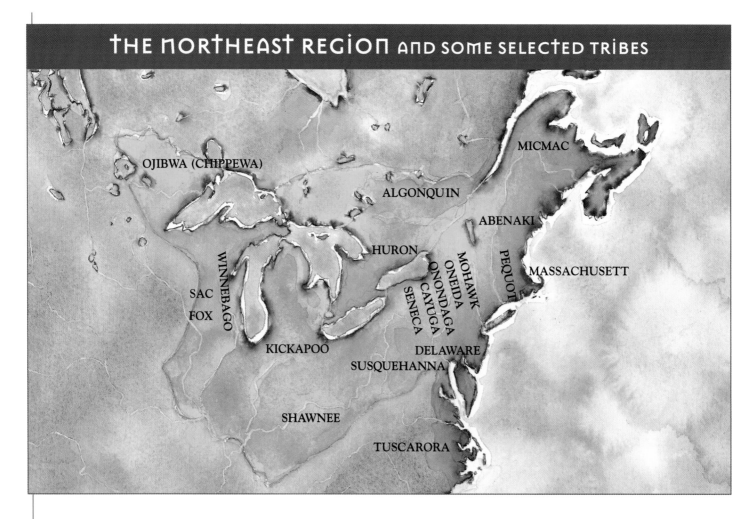

THE NORTHEAST REGION stretches from the Great Lakes in the west to the Atlantic Ocean in the east. It is an area of lakes, rivers, and dense woodlands. Several mountain ranges run from north to south, creating barriers to easy travel.

The people who lived in the Northeast were primarily hunters and fishermen, but they also ate a variety of wild plants, roots, and berries. Wild rice was an important food to some of the eastern Indians, especially those who lived near the Great Lakes. Many of the Indians in this region were also farmers. Among the foods they planted were squash, pumpkins, beans, and corn.

Another thing the Indians of the Northeast had in common was language. Although they spoke many different languages, most of these languages belonged to one of two language groups or families: the Algonquian and the Iroquoian. A few tribes, such as the Winnebago, who lived on the western edge of this region, spoke the Siouan language, which means that they once were closely related to the tribes of the Great Plains known as the Sioux.

The Northeast region was dominated by the Iroquois. Contrary to what many people believe, the Iroquois were not a tribe but a group of tribes that joined together to form what was known as the

THE PEOPLE OF THE LONGHOUSE

ACCORDING TO IROQUOIS tradition, the five tribes living in what is now New York State were once locked in a bloody and senseless war. After heeding the message of a holy man who urged the tribes to stop their endless warring, a Mohawk warrior named Hiawatha took it upon himself to visit each of the warring tribes and invite their leaders to a great gathering to arrange a peace. At the conference the leaders of the five tribes agreed to "hold hands so tightly that a falling tree could not separate them." These tribes were the C a y u g a , M o h a w k , O n o n d a g a , Oneida, and S e n e c a . Together they formed the Iroquois Confederacy. (Later, a sixth tribe, the Tuscarora, joined the confederacy.)

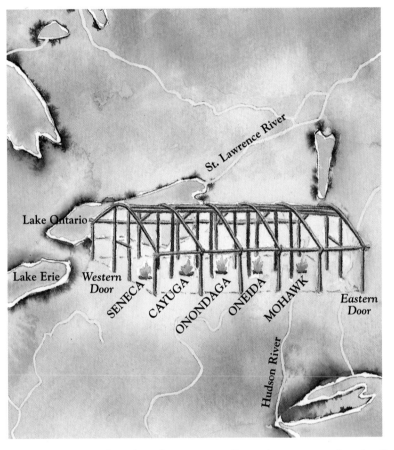

The five nations of the confederacy occupied a huge area from the Hudson River in the east to Lake Erie in the west. Their homeland resembled an enormous rectangle. As part of their agreement, the tribes divided their territory into five side-by-side strips of land, each governed by its own tribal council. A continuously burning ceremonial fire marked the site of each council. The smoke from the five council fires rising into the air resembled the smoke seen from the fires found in an Iroquois longhouse.

In this symbolic longhouse, the Seneca were the keepers of the Western Door, since they were the westernmost of the five tribes in the confederacy. The Mohawks were the keepers of the Eastern Door. The other tribes were arranged in between like the families and fires in an ordinary longhouse. It was agreed that the Onondagas, the tribe in the center, would be the "fire keepers" and that future conferences would be held at Onondaga. The Onondagas were also the "wampum keepers" of the confederacy.

The Iroquois called themselves the People of the Longhouse or the People of the Five Fires. They later called the thirteen original colonies of the United States the People of the Thirteen Fires.

Iroquois Confederacy (see page 53). The confederacy worked so well that the founding fathers of the United States may have used it as a model in developing a plan for linking the original thirteen colonies into a united country.

The Iroquois Confederacy was governed by a council of fifty sachems, or chiefs. To ensure that they did not dominate the confederacy, the Seneca, which was the largest tribe, had the fewest sachems: eight. The smallest tribe, the Onondaga, had the most sachems: fourteen. The Cayuga had ten, and the Mohawk and Oneida each had nine sachems.

The position of sachem was inherited and could only be held by a man—although a woman could act in place of a boy until he was old enough to take his place at the council. Each sachem had a name and each one had a specific duty or set of duties. For example, one sachem was known as Keeper of the Longhouse.

Another sachem was known as Keeper of the Council Wampum. Wampum was a tube-shaped bead made from the shells of clams. It was made in two colors: purple, which was very rare, and white. Indians of the Northeast used wampum as a sort of money and for ceremonial purposes. Among the tribes of the Iroquois Confederacy, belts made of wampum were used to carry messages and also as a badge to identify tribal ambassadors.

The Iroquois were very warlike. They did not fight with other members of the confederacy, of course, but they fought against other tribes. To strike at an enemy, Iroquois war parties might travel hundreds of miles and be away from home for weeks

▶ *An Iroquois war club.*

▼ *Half of a wampum belt presented to the Wyandot by the Seneca Indians. It was traditional for the tribe presenting a belt like this to keep half of it. Running along the bottom of this belt is half of a beaver symbol made from purple clamshells.*

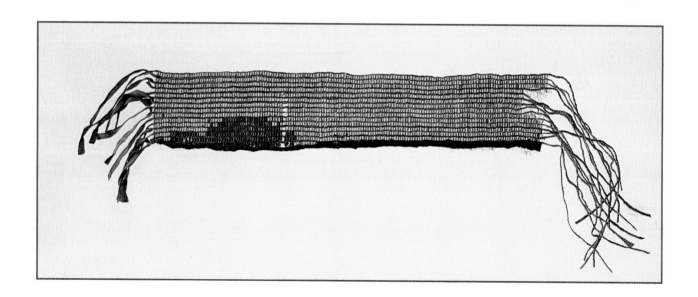

at a time. Iroquois men and boys spent a great deal of time training and preparing themselves for battle. They carved special war clubs with balls on the end and they became expert marksmen with the bow and arrow. Few Iroquois lived to old age because so many were killed or captured in battle. To make up for the men they lost in battle, the Iroquois would "adopt" young boys they captured from enemy villages.

Scalps—small patches of hair cut from the head of an enemy killed in battle—were prized trophies of war. More highly prized were prisoners. The Iroquois tested the bravery of some of their prisoners by torturing them until they died. However, many prisoners were taken back to the Iroquois villages and adopted.

Iroquois villages were very large. They were usually built along streams or lakes on a flat piece of land at the top of a steep hill. The hill gave protection from attack and the Iroquois usually built a wall of logs around the entire village. The villages were used all year long. The men would leave the villages to go hunting and fishing. The women would tend nearby garden plots, where they grew corn, beans, and squash, which the Iroquois called the "three sisters."

The "three sisters" was a symbolic term. It also stood for women, the household, and the continuity of Iroquois society, which to the Iroquois were one and the same. Although men governed the

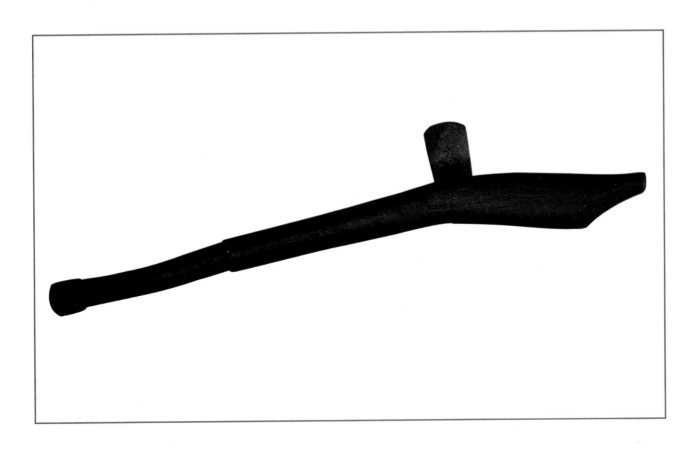

TRADE NETWORKS

LONG BEFORE THE arrival of Europeans, the various Indian tribes of North America had considerable contact with one another through the exchange of foods, gifts, and objects of barter, or trade. The continent of North America was laced with trade routes. Following these routes, some objects traveled only as far as the next village; others traveled hundreds and even thousands of miles from their point of origin.

Usually, a tribe would trade products with a neighboring tribe. This tribe, in turn, might exchange those products with another neighbor farther away. The farther an object traveled from its point of origin, the more valuable it became.

Dentalium shells, for example, were highly prized by many tribes for use in necklaces and earrings and for other decorative purposes. The source of these thin, tubelike shells was the west coast of Vancouver Island on the Pacific, yet they were used by Indians as far away as the upper Missouri River in the Dakotas.

The Northeast tribes enjoyed well-established trade routes along the many lakes and rivers of the region. Indians in canoes were able to travel quickly over great distances. Copper from Lake Superior was traded with tribes on the Atlantic coast for wampum and tobacco. Minnesota red stone, which the Indians used in making their tobacco pipes, was traded to tribes as far away as present-day New York.

The extent of the trade networks in North America can be seen from archaeological work being done at Cahokia. This was a great city of the Mississippian culture located where St. Louis, Missouri, is today. Although little is known of the people who built Cahokia, it is clear that they were great traders. Among the objects that have been found there are sheets of copper from the Great Lakes, arrowheads made from the black chert found in Oklahoma, decorated shells from the Gulf of Mexico, pieces of mica from North Carolina, and stone from Wyoming. The trade network of Cahokia covered an area larger than Europe.

Iroquois, the women controlled daily life. Women owned the garden plots and the houses. Iroquois inherited their clans and possessions through their mothers. When an Iroquois man married, he joined his wife's family and went to live in her longhouse.

Longhouses were built of young trees called saplings and were covered with large pieces of bark from the elm tree. They were about 25 feet wide and could be as long as 200 feet, although usually they were much shorter. The average longhouse was about 80 feet long and was home to many families. An aisle containing fire pits ran down the middle. Each fire pit was shared by two families, one on each side of the aisle.

A family had a section of the longhouse about 25 feet in length for its own use. The families living in a longhouse were all related to each other through the mothers or wives. As more families joined a longhouse, they would add new sections to the ends. That is why some longhouses got very long indeed.

Each family, usually a father and mother and several children, had platforms about a foot off the ground along the edge of their section. At night they slept on the platforms. During the day they sat on them. Above the platforms were shelves for clothes, weapons, baskets, and other household goods. There might also be storage bins for corn and other foods.

Inside the entrances at either end of the longhouse were stacks of firewood for people to use as needed. Smoke from the fires escaped through holes in the roof above the fire pits. Because longhouses were usually dark and smoky inside, families preferred spending much of their time outdoors.

The Iroquois made their clothes from tanned deerskins decorated with dyed porcupine quills. Tools such as mortars and pestles, used to grind corn, were made of wood. Baskets and other containers were made of bark. Because there were so many

▼ *Beaded headdresses from the Cayuga (top and bottom) and Oneida tribes.*

▼ *Beaded moccasins from various tribes of the Iroquois Confederacy.*

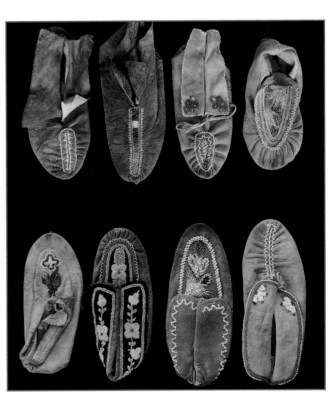

▲ *An Iroquois man paddles a canoe. Canoes like this could be up to 25 feet long. The frames were made of cedar and the skin from birch bark sewn together with roots and waterproofed with resin from trees.*

▶ *Iroquois container, made from the bark of an elm tree.*

rivers and lakes in Iroquois country, the men made canoes for fishing and traveling. The preferred material for making canoes was the bark of the paper birch tree.

Iroquois life involved many ceremonies and rituals. An important one was the Green Corn Festival, which the Iroquois celebrated at the time when the corn was ready to harvest and eat. Many tribes in the East, such as the Cherokee, had similar ceremonies. As part of the festival the Iroquois would dance, give speeches of thanksgiving, burn tobacco (a sacred plant to many Indians), and say prayers like this one, which some Seneca still use

▲ *An Iroquois mask made from corn husks. Masks like this were worn by dancers during ceremonies held at the beginning of the year to ensure a good harvest. This one has small bags of tobacco sewn into the forehead.*

when thanking the creator for a rich harvest:

> *Great Spirit, listen to us.*
> *We thank you for your great goodness*
> *in causing our mother, the earth,*
> *again to bring forth her fruits.*
> *Great Spirit, the council here assembled,*
> *the aged men and women,*
> *the strong warriors, the women and children,*
> *unite their voice of thanksgiving to you.*

Prayer was important to the Iroquois, as it is to all American Indian peoples. They believed in a supreme being who brought good luck and health to his people.

Although the Iroquois used more than two hundred plants to cure sickness, protect themselves from insect bites, and stay healthy, they also believed strongly in the

▲ ▶ *False Face masks from the Cayuga (above)*
and Seneca tribes.

power of prayers and rituals to cure illness. Members of an Iroquois society called the False Faces represented spirits who were known to cure various sicknesses. Wearing intricately carved wooden masks, the members of the False Faces society would creep into the house of a sick person. They shook rattles made from the shells of snapping turtles, made strange and scary sounds, and sprinkled ashes on their patients so as to frighten away the spirits that caused the illness. As payment for these services, the False Faces received gifts of tobacco and food.

◆

The Indians of the Northeast first met Europeans in 1534, little more than forty years after Columbus came to the Americas, when the French explorer Jacques Cartier visited the St. Lawrence River. Because they were well organized, powerful, and warlike, the Indians of the Northeast played a major role in the history of the region for more than two hundred years (see sidebar). But by the time of the American Revolution, war and the pressure from Europeans settling in their homeland had taken its toll on the Iroquois. As a result of the Revolution, the Iroquois Confederacy disintegrated. Some of its people moved north to Canada. Those who remained were forced to live on reservations, some far from their homeland—some of the Oneidas, for example, now live on a reservation in Wisconsin. Other Iroquois remain in Canada and a few still live in New York.

FRENCH AND BRITISH ALLIANCES

THE INDIANS OF North America usually welcomed the first Europeans they met. The strangers from across the sea had things that Indians wanted: iron axes and knives, guns, cloth, beads, and brass kettles were obviously superior to the stone tools and wooden weapons that the Indians possessed. They offered the Europeans furs, baskets, food, and other items in exchange for these products. Soon Indians and Europeans on the Atlantic and the Pacific coasts were actively engaged in trade.

However, when the European nations began competing among themselves for control of North America, their rivalry disrupted this relationship. The primary opponents were Britain and France. Both countries formed alliances with the Indian tribes that lived near their colonies along the Atlantic coast. The French, who settled in what is now Canada, allied themselves with the dominant tribes in eastern Canada, the Hurons and the Algonquins. The British became allies with the powerful Iroquois Confederacy.

The rivalry between Britain and France at first benefited their Indian allies. In recognition of their loyalty, Indian leaders received medals, flags, and uniforms from the monarchs of France and England. They were invited overseas to the royal courts, where they had their portraits painted and were treated like kings. The Indians got higher prices for the beaver skins and other furs they traded to the Europeans. The tribes enjoyed a short period of prosperity.

In the long run, however, the rivalries between European nations were harmful to the Indians. Between 1689 and 1763, Britain and France fought four great wars over America, which ultimately resulted in a British victory. So many warriors died in these wars that the Hurons and the Algonquins were destroyed and the Iroquois Confederacy eventually disintegrated.

▼ *This woodcut from 1758, a few years before the French and Indian Wars ended, shows figures representing England and France struggling for the loyalty of the Indians.*

PRÆVALEBIT ÆQUIOR.

5

THE NORTHWEST:
A HAIDA PLANKHOUSE

This Haida house is home to several families. The owner is a wealthy person who can afford valuable wood carvings like those on the post supporting the house roof and elaborate clothes like the beautiful blankets decorated with buttons made from mother-of-pearl. A large pit in the center of the house holds the fire that provides warmth and is used for cooking meals. The people with the

lowest status in the house live on this bottom level, next to the fire. On the top floor, level with the ground outside, live the house owner and other nobles.

THE NORTHWEST REGION
AND SOME SELECTED TRIBES

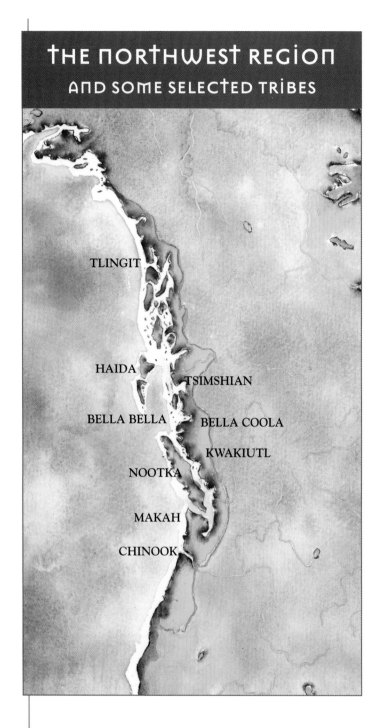

TLINGIT

HAIDA

TSIMSHIAN

BELLA BELLA

BELLA COOLA

KWAKIUTL

NOOTKA

MAKAH

CHINOOK

THE NORTHWEST COAST region is shaped like a long, narrow arc that extends for 1,500 miles along the northern Pacific coast from southern Oregon to the Gulf of Alaska. The climate is mild and pleasant, although rain falls frequently throughout the year. The summers are cool. The winters are warm and wet.

The Indians who lived along the Northwest Coast were isolated and protected from other people by the Pacific Ocean to the west and a series of high, broad mountain ranges to the east. As a result, they developed a culture quite different from other native North Americans. They did not have to work very hard to get enough to eat because the ocean and the region's many rivers and forests supplied plenty of food. The forests also provided timber. The Indians of the Northwest Coast were great woodcarvers and they made many things of giant proportions. These included canoes, totem poles, and vast houses. With just a single giant room capable of holding a hundred or more people, these houses were the largest of any in native North America.

The people of the Northwest Coast hunted whales, seals, sea lions, otters, and other marine mammals, but fish were their

▶ *Magnificent wooden masks like these were worn during dances held by secret societies throughout the Northwest.*

Top left: Haida mask representing the face of a fish.

Center left: Haida shark costume. The head was worn as a mask and the back and fin were attached to the body of the dancer with a belt.

Bottom left: Haida deer's head mask.

Top right: Kwakiutl raven mask.

Center right: Haida sparrow hawk mask, decorated with feathers.

Bottom right: Bella Bella mask, part human, part eagle.

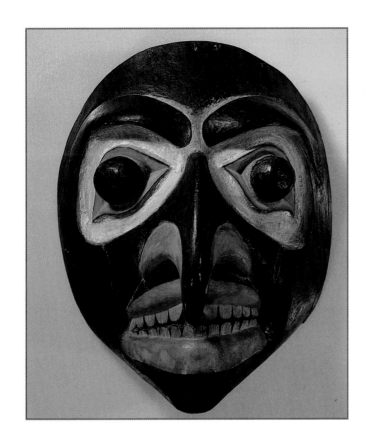

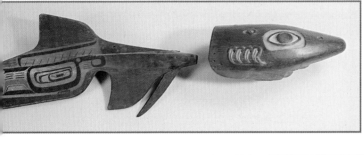

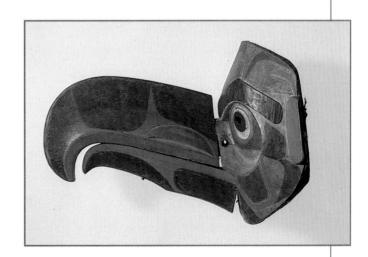

most important food. Fish were everywhere. The favorite was the salmon, found in almost every river along the coast. The largest salmon weighed 80 pounds or more.

Another important fish was halibut, which are even bigger than salmon. Some weigh more than 300 pounds. To catch such large fish, the Indians made hooks out of wood and used pieces of bone as the barbs.

When the Indians got tired of eating fish, they could sample shellfish such as clams, mussels, oysters, scallops, and crabs. The shell of another shellfish, the dentalium, was used to decorate their clothes and to make necklaces and earrings.

The Northwest Coast Indians also had lots of animals, birds, and plants to eat. In the forests were deer, bears, and elk, while thousands upon thousands of birds lived and nested along the coastline and on the rivers. The Indians ate the meat or eggs of as many as twenty-six different kinds of water birds, including loons, swans, ducks, and geese. They also ate herbs, roots, berries, and seaweed.

For woodwork, the Indians liked to use red cedar, a type of tree that is abundant in the region. The red cedar is a forest giant. Its wood is light and strong and resists decay. It was easily split with stone and wood tools into large, thin boards, ideal for using as planks for houses. Even its bark was important: the outer bark, which can

be removed in large sheets, served as shingles for the roofs of houses. The inner bark, either twisted or cut into strips, was used for making capes, baskets, mats, twine, and blankets. When shredded, the inner bark also served nicely as baby diapers.

The most impressive use of wood by the Northwest Coast Indians was in the making of canoes, totem poles, and masks. Northwest Coast canoes were boats of great beauty and size—as much as 40 feet long and capable of holding forty people. The totem poles, which are really decorated tree trunks, were even more spectacular. Using simple tools made of stone, shell, and the front teeth of beavers, Northwest Coast artists carved and painted strange and wonderful figures representing real people, animals, birds, and fish, as well as imaginary creatures. These carvings told stories that the Indians could "read" like books, starting at the top of the pole and moving toward the bottom (see page 70). The men who made totem poles were skilled carvers who often traveled from village to village carving poles for important people or for special occasions. They were well paid for their work, because totem poles took a long time to carve.

When a totem pole was completed, the owner would usually host a celebration called a potlatch. The potlatch was a party like none other in native North America. Visitors would come from miles away and

▶ *Using wedges and stone-headed sledgehammers, Haida men cut planks from a live tree. Several planks could be cut this way without killing the tree.*

TOTEM POLES

THE INDIANS OF the Northwest Coast are famous for gigantic carvings made from the trunks of cedar trees, popularly known as totem poles. Artisans of the Northwest Coast tribes such as the Haida, Kwakiutl, and Tlingit continue to create these wonderful works of art to this day.

Totem poles varied from as little as 10 feet to as much as 80 feet in length. Most had several faces carved on them. Some of these came from the natural world, such as beavers and grizzly bears, birds such as eagles and ravens, and sea creatures such as salmon and orcas. Some were composed of parts taken from different animals. Others were entirely imaginary or came from the supernatural world. Stylized designs represented certain creatures. For example, a thunderbird was carved with widely spread wings and a curved beak. The beaver was represented by its two big front teeth. A bird with a long, sharp beak was the raven, while the orca was identified by its distinctive dorsal fin.

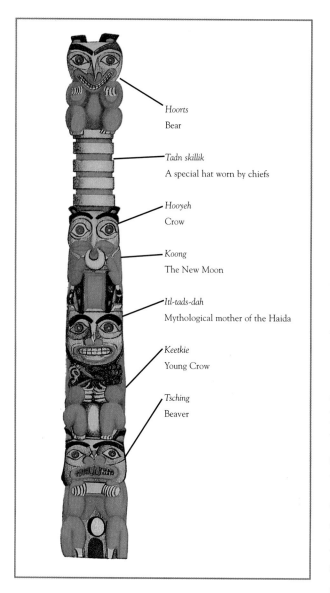

Hoorts
Bear

Tadn skillik
A special hat worn by chiefs

Hooyeh
Crow

Koong
The New Moon

Itl-tads-dah
Mythological mother of the Haida

Keetkie
Young Crow

Tsching
Beaver

Some totem poles told a story like a folktale. Others commemorated an important person, family, or event. Some were made to poke fun at people, like a person who failed to pay a debt. Many told the story of an important person's family, with the carved creatures on the pole representing his lineage. These poles served the same function as the coat of arms a knight in medieval Europe carried on his shield.

Some totem poles were used as entrances to a chief's house. Others might be used to support the roof. Some served as grave markers and even had coffins at the top.

The pole shown here formed the door of a Haida house. Above the door is Beaver. On his head sits the figure of Itl-tads-dah, the mythological mother of the Haida tribe, holding a young crow. Above her is Crow, holding the new moon in his beak. The circles above Crow represent the hat worn by Haida chiefs, and on top sits Bear. A legend associated with this carving tells how Beaver ate the moon and, seeing this, Itl-tads-dah sent Crow to find the new moon and bring it home in his beak. Meanwhile, Bear watches to see that all goes well. ■

might stay for days or weeks at a time. The carvings on the totem pole would be explained to the visitors and then there would be much feasting, drumming, dancing, and singing. The dancers wore colorful blankets and wooden masks that resembled birds' heads with long beaks or the heads of fish or other animals. Each performer danced alone, his steps and arm movements mimicking the creature on his mask.

The host of a potlatch and his family not only had to feed the visitors, but also give them valuable presents. The more valuable the presents given away, the more prestige the host enjoyed. Sometimes the host and his family gave away everything they owned in order to impress their guests with their generosity.

One of the finest gifts to be given away was called a copper. This was a large sheet of beaten copper that looked like a shield with painted symbols. Some coppers had names—for example, Sea Lion, Beaver Face, Too Great a Whale, or the Copper All Other Coppers Are Ashamed to Look At. Coppers had no practical use—they were simply symbols of wealth, to be displayed in their owners' homes or given away at a potlatch.

Besides celebrating a new totem pole, potlatches would be given to honor important visitors from other tribes, the building of a new house, or the naming of a new chief.

Many different tribes lived along the Northwest Coast, speaking as many as forty distinct languages. Some of the better-known Northwest Coast tribes are the Tlingit, the Makah, the Kwakiutl, and the Haida.

The Haida lived on what are known today as the Queen Charlotte Islands. They called their homeland Haida Gwai. Haida Gwai consisted of two large islands and 150 smaller ones that lie from 50 to 80 miles off the coast of British Columbia.

▲ *A Haida copper, decorated with its owner's clan crest.*

Everyone in Haida society had specific roles or duties. According to a Haida saying, "Every woman needs a digging stick. Every man needs a fishing line." Women and girls gathered roots, berries, and seaweed for food, collected cedar bark and spruce roots for weaving, and processed

▲ *A ceremonial Haida chief's hat decorated with a carved bear, the chief's clan symbol.*

▼ *A ceremonial blanket called a Chilkat blanket, belonging to a Tlingit Indian chief. The images on the blanket represent the chief's clan.*

and preserved food items. They tanned animal skins and made clothing and blankets. Men and boys fished and hunted. They built houses. They carved and painted masks, canoes, and totem poles.

Haida families valued their children—especially girls, because Haida society was "matrilineal," which means that the family line was passed on through daughters, not sons. Children got their names at birth at a small feast, but they could be given additional names later in life when their fathers held potlatches. Babies were believed to be reincarnations of someone who had died in the past.

Girls learned Haida customs and crafts from their mothers. Boys were taught not by their fathers, but by their mother's brothers. Boys had to swim in ice-cold water in the wintertime because their uncles believed this would make them strong. They ate dragonfly wings because it was believed this made them fast swimmers, and they sucked the tongues of diving ducks because it was believed this would help them hold their breath underwater for a long time.

The Haida picked the sites for their villages very carefully—close to halibut fishing, to fresh drinking water, to shellfish, and to a beach suitable for landing their canoes. A safe, secluded harbor provided protection from storms and from enemies. The Haida were a warlike people. They traveled long distances in their canoes to raid the villages of other Northwest Coast tribes to capture people to use as slaves and to get valuable booty such as food and furs, or to take revenge for previous attacks.

Haida plankhouses were made of wood. They were very large and were often home to several related families. In the center of the house was a fireplace in a large pit; a hole in the roof above the fireplace allowed smoke to escape. The insides of the houses were dug deep into the ground and had several levels. In the bottom level, next to the fireplace, slept the slaves, who were the lowest-ranking people in Northwest Coast society. The highest level, even with the ground outside, was reserved for nobles—the heads of the families or clans, who were known as the house chiefs.

At the front of each house stood a large totem pole. The carvings told visitors the clan of the people who lived in the house. Common clan crests were the raven, the killer whale or orca, and the eagle. When

▼ *This housefront was made by the Haida's neighbors on the mainland, the Tsimshian. It shows the figure of Naquanaks, the Tsimshian "chief of the seas," above the door, with a whale on each side.*

visitors arrived at a strange village, the poles helped them find the house in which they would be most welcome. A member of the eagle clan, for example, would look for a house with an eagle at the top of the pole. Sometimes visitors entered the house through a hole in the mouth or the stomach of the creature at the bottom of the pole. Large and important Haida houses even had their own names—for example, the House Where One Always May Expect Food, the House That Other Chiefs Like to Peek At, and the House Where People Always Like to Go.

◆

The Haida did not meet Europeans until 1774, when the Spanish explorer Juan

▲ ▶ *A photograph of the Haida village of Skedans in the Queen Charlotte Islands, taken several decades after the village had been abandoned. On the right is an artist's impression of what the village might have looked like when it was occupied.*

▼ *A Tlingit rattle in the shape of a duck. Rattles like this one were used by shamans when healing sick people.*

Pérez reached Haida Gwai. Because the Haida lived so far out to sea, they did not have many more European visitors until the nineteenth century. At first they welcomed the Europeans, who brought them iron tools that made it easier to build their houses and carve their totem poles and canoes. But the Europeans also brought diseases. The worst was smallpox. At the time of Pérez's visit there were perhaps 10,000 Haida; by 1915 smallpox had killed so many that only 588 remained. Many of their villages had to be abandoned.

Since 1915, the Haida population has grown. They still live on the Queen Charlotte Islands. Like the other peoples of the Northwest Coast, they still love the sea and they love to create their wonderful carvings, which are valued by museums and collectors of Indian art.

TRADE WITH RUSSIA

FOR 126 YEARS, Alaska was part of the Russian empire. Russia based its claim on the exploits of the Danish-born explorer Vitus Bering, who crossed into Alaska from Siberia in 1741. He was followed by Siberian fur hunters, who crossed over to the Aleutian Islands, reaching Kodiak Island in 1762. After conquering the Aleuts, an Indian tribe in the area, the hunters began trading with peoples on the Northwest Coast as far south as California.

Russia's fur trade with North America grew steadily. An important step was the establishment of the Russian-American

This Russian medal was found in a Pomo grave in northern California— evidence of Russian trading along the Pacific coast of North America.

Company in 1781, which brought the fur trade under Russian government control—and brought an end to the brutality that many Indians had experienced at the hands of the Siberian fur traders. The headquarters of the Russian-American Company was a post named St. Michael the Archangel, built on Sitka Island in 1799. Located among the Tlingit Indians, St. Michael became an important agricultural and trade center for the Indians living on the Alaskan mainland. From Sitka, the Russians continued to move south along the Pacific coast. In 1812 they built Fort Ross, located only 90 miles from San Francisco Bay. Fort Ross was the only non-Spanish settlement built by Europeans in early California.

The Russians at Fort Ross enjoyed friendly relations with the nearby Pomo Indians. Like the Tlingit on Sitka, the Pomo grew food for the Russians, and some of them learned to speak Russian and became converts to the Russian Orthodox religion.

Because the Russians were interested only in trade and not in claiming Indian lands, the two groups got along well. The native peoples were considered citizens of the Russian empire. Their support enabled Russia to maintain a presence in North America until 1867, when the Russian government decided to sell Alaska to the United States. The end of the Russian regime shocked the Indians of the Northwest Coast, who had come to rely on Russian trade goods and friendship.

POTLATCH BY FAITH WILLIAMS

I was raised in Alaska in a small town of five hundred people. The Athapaskan Indians who lived there made up about 40 percent of the population and were scattered throughout the town. However, a small number of Indian families lived in the Village, which was located alongside the river at one end of town.

The Indians who lived in the Village spent the better part of the summer fishing and processing salmon for sale and for their own use. Now, while there are jobs in summer, many Villagers still live a subsistence lifestyle, meaning they hunt and fish and gather berries and mushrooms to supplement the very expensive items purchased from the local grocery store or from shopping centers in the city, 60 miles away. Many Indians in Alaska still live this way, using food resources they can hunt, fish, or gather in their regions.

For our meat diets, we hunted moose, ducks, geese, ptarmigan, and other birds and set snares for rabbits. Fish were plentiful in the rivers and streams, and we gathered blueberries, cranberries, and mushrooms for winter use. We grew a large garden and preserved root vegetables such as potatoes, turnips, carrots, and onions in our dirt basement.

No matter how little food might be available, sharing is a very important element of our Indian culture. Whether we are visiting at someone's fish camp in the summer or making a trip to the Village to purchase fish, we are always invited for tea and something delectable to eat—smoked salmon with a pilot boy cracker, for example. Even today, my mother has what she calls an Indian Tea Party with her great-granddaughters, consisting of tea with honey and smoked fish.

One of the more important ways in which the Indians share food is at a potlatch. A potlatch is a gathering of the tribe to celebrate with food, dance, honoring, and sharing. Traditional foods such as smoked and frozen fish, duck and other game birds, and berries are donated by the Villagers. Men of the Village will hunt for fresh meat, such as moose, for soups and roasts. Vegetable dishes, salads, and desserts supplement the food table. After the eating is finished, the hall is cleared for dances. Everyone is invited to join in the dancing, which often goes on into the wee hours of the morning.

I remember clearly a potlatch that was held after a big tribal meeting to celebrate with visitors for the Christmas holidays. I had returned home from the city, where I was attending college. I walked into the communal hall and my mother told me that Chief Alexander (we called him Grandpa Frank) wanted to speak with me. When I walked over to him, he motioned me to sit in his chair and he sat on the floor beside me. You see, chairs were for the chief, council members, elders, and honored guests. Everyone else—adults, children, and teens—knelt on the floor in front of oil-paper strips that lined the hall. I was very embarrassed to be put in the limelight and extremely surprised by the chief's actions. I realized I was being honored as a young person who had left the Village and honored the people with my achievements.

As the food was passed, all the traditional dishes were passed to the elders first. Special efforts were always taken to note the desires and tastes of honored guests. Special and sometimes scarce delicacies were shared with them, even if it meant others went without. When the dried white-fish—one of my favorite, and usually not very plentiful, treats—was passed, the chief motioned for it to come to me first. This was a very unselfish gesture and one that filled me with pride and gratitude.

Faith Williams is now retired after twenty-two years of service for the United States Senate and the Departments of Energy and the Interior. She and her husband live in Luray, Virginia, on twenty acres of wooded and pastured land that she says is as close as she can get to a simulation of her beloved Alaska. Her family, who all live in Alaska, includes her daughter and two granddaughters.

6

THE GREAT PLAINS: A SIOUX TIPI

A Sioux camp on the Great Plains. Inside the tipi sits a group of older women working dyed porcupine quills. Outside, one woman mashes berries in a dish made of animal hide while another holds her baby in a cradle decorated with beads. The baskets and other tools are typical of those used by the Plains Indians: lightweight and easy to carry, and beautifully decorated. The buffalo-hide tipi cover in the background is

decorated with battle scenes reflecting the importance of its owner. New buffalo hides are staked out on the ground to dry before being tanned. Farther in the background, women erect a tipi as a family arrives at the camp carrying their belongings on a horse-drawn travois made of tipi poles.

THE GREAT PLAINS AND SOME SELECTED TRIBES

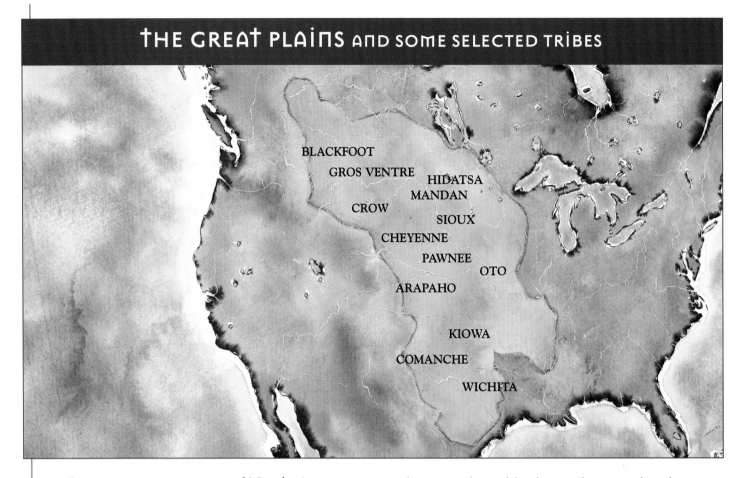

BLACKFOOT
GROS VENTRE
HIDATSA
MANDAN
CROW
SIOUX
CHEYENNE
PAWNEE
OTO
ARAPAHO
KIOWA
COMANCHE
WICHITA

IN THE HEARTLAND of North America is a vast area known as the Great Plains. This flat, almost treeless region reaches more than 2,000 miles, from the Saskatchewan River in the north to the Rio Grande in the south. To the west it is bounded by the Rocky Mountains; to the east it spills across the Missouri River and merges with the midwestern prairies. It is a grassy land of wind and sun that once supported millions of large, shaggy mammals called bison.

The bison—or buffalo, as it is popularly known—was the lifeblood of the Indians who lived on the Great Plains. It fed them physically and spiritually. It gave them most of their food. It gave them their homes, their blankets, their tools, their ornaments—even their toys, all of which were made from parts of the dead animal. Men, women, and children carried good luck charms that looked like buffaloes.

Much of the religious life of the Plains

▲ *The tough hide of the buffalo was used by Plains Indians to make shields. This Sioux shield has a buckskin cover decorated with a painted dragonfly, symbolizing the warrior's ability to elude the enemy.*

Indians revolved around the buffalo. When they died, they expected to go to a land in the hereafter crowded with buffaloes. Some Indians believed the Milky Way—the trail of stars that dominates the nighttime sky—was the dust raised by the buffalo herds of the spirit world.

Although the Great Plains teemed with wildlife, for thousands of years few native peoples lived there. Most tribes in the region were like the Mandan, who lived in permanent villages along the edge of the plains and ventured upon them only once or twice a year to hunt buffaloes and other animals such as antelope, deer, and elk. After a hunt they returned to their villages, which were usually along rivers, where they planted corn and other crops and felt secure from their enemies.

The coming of the horse changed all this. Although horses had once lived in North and South America, they had been extinct there for thousands of years until Christopher Columbus brought them back to the New World in 1493. Over the next two hundred years, horses made their way from Mexico to the Great Plains, where they were embraced by many tribes. Before

▼ *Plains Indians were daring, skillful hunters. This painting by George Catlin shows Comanches armed with bows and arrows and lances hunting buffaloes from horseback.*

the horse the only beast of burden the Indians had was the dog.

On foot, the Indians could not travel very far or very fast. Hunting buffaloes was difficult and dangerous. But with horses the Plains Indians could move swiftly. They could follow the buffalo herds, which meant they usually had plenty of meat to eat, as well as hides for making clothing, robes, and tents.

As a result, certain tribes completely changed their way of life. The Cheyenne and Crow, for example, stopped farming and moved from their original homes near the Great Lakes to the plains so they could follow the buffalo all year round. The Comanche, who had formerly lived a harsh and precarious life in the Rocky Mountains as hunter-gatherers, also moved onto the plains, where they became full-time buffalo hunters—and perhaps the finest horsemen the world has ever known. Other tribes that moved onto the Great Plains in the centuries after Europeans arrived in the Americas included the Sioux, Arapaho, Kiowa, Gros Ventre, and Blackfoot.

The Teton Sioux, or Lakota, as they prefer to be called, are representative of the Plains Indians. Originally they lived in what is today Minnesota and eastern South Dakota, but they moved onto the plains about the middle of the eighteenth century, when they learned to ride and were able to obtain enough horses to change their lifestyle. Speaking the Siouan language, they were a numerous people consisting of seven bands, or sub-tribes, among them the Oglala, Brulé, and Hunkpapa. Although Sioux families often owned many horses, a warrior usually had one that was special to him. It would be a handsome, spirited horse—obedient, swift, and fearless—which was used only for hunting buffaloes or riding into battle. The owner kept it near him always, even at night. While asleep, he kept one end of a rope tied to his wrist; the other end went under the tipi cover and was tied to the horse.

Sioux warriors risked their lives to capture such fine horses. A young warrior would creep into an enemy village at night, try to cut the rope without waking the horse's owner, and then quietly lead the horse out of the village. Once he was a safe distance away, he would mount the horse and race for home. When he got there, the warrior would often give his valuable prize away, usually to a woman whose husband had died or to a family that had no horses. This would show everyone in his village that the young man was as generous as he was brave.

Such a feat was called a coup (pronounced "coo") and was one of a series of war honors known among the Sioux and certain other Plains tribes as "counting coup." Other coups were earned for other acts of heroism, such as touching an

THE HORSE AND THE GUN

FEW THINGS INTRODUCED by Europeans changed the way of life of America's native peoples more than the horse and the gun. Although the horse originated in the Americas more than 40 million years ago, it had become extinct in its homeland. The people of America either walked or used boats. It took them a long time to move from place to place.

Christopher Columbus brought 25 horses to the Americas on his second voyage in 1493. For almost two centuries, the Spanish tried to keep Indians from owning horses. They knew that the horse would give Indians a powerful tool for protecting their land from invasion. But in 1680, the pueblo Indians in New Mexico drove the Spanish out of their country.

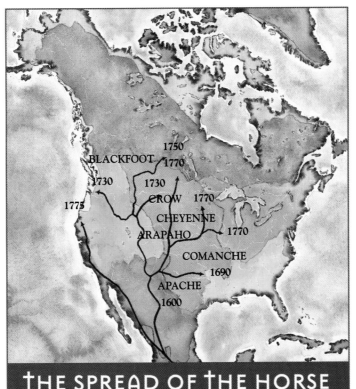

Left behind were thousands of horses. Some the pueblo Indians traded to neighboring tribes. Others ran away and started huge herds of wild horses that came to be known as mustangs. From New Mexico, horses moved rapidly north and east along the trading networks that existed between the various tribes.

Everywhere the horse went it shocked and surprised the Indians, who had never seen an animal that could carry a person. Many thought the horse was a large dog. For example, the Blackfoot word for horse is *ponokomita*, meaning "elk-dog." Nonetheless, the horse transformed the lives of many tribes, giving them mobility and a powerful weapon for hunting and waging war.

Meanwhile, guns were moving west from New England. The English, Dutch, and French began trading and selling guns to the Indians, even though they knew that Indians with guns would become a formidable foe in battle. As the eastern tribes got guns, they began to make war on their neighbors to the west, who had no guns.

The horse and the gun met in the center of North America, on the Great Plains. Tribes such as the Sioux, the Cheyenne, and the Crow got guns from the east and the horse from the west. The result was the mounted plains warrior who became a much-feared fighter in the nineteenth century.

▲ Four magnificent feather headdresses. From left to right: Arapaho, Blackfoot, Cheyenne, and Sioux.

enemy in battle, capturing a weapon from an enemy, or not retreating during a fight. By counting coups, warriors earned the right to wear eagle feathers in their war bonnets. Some warriors became so distinguished for their war deeds that they wore eagle-feather war bonnets with trailers that stretched almost to the ground.

As hunters and warriors, the Sioux depended on speed and mobility for survival. Everything they owned had to be durable, lightweight, and easily carried. The best example of this was the tipi, which was the perfect home for Plains Indians.

Tipis were cone-shaped tents made of buffalo skins supported by poles made from lodgepole pine trees. They were easy to make, simple to erect, and could be folded into a compact bundle. Tipis were made in various sizes depending upon the number of people living in them, but usually they were between 12 and 16 feet across at the base and made from eight to twelve buffalo skins that had been carefully tanned and sewn tightly together. The front of the tent was laced together by means of small wooden or bone pegs. In the wintertime the base of the tent would be held down with rocks, but in the summertime the sides were often rolled up a few feet for ventilation. To keep the tent warm in the wintertime, some families made a liner of deerskin or elk skin. This would be attached to the tipi poles on the inside and hung straight down to the ground. Grass and brush stuffed between the tipi liner and the outside of the tent provided further insulation. Tipis, although snug and warm in even the coldest weather, could be a little smoky. The fireplace was in the center of the tent directly beneath a smoke hole. Two flaps made from the ears of a buffalo covered the hole and could be opened or closed by means of long poles.

Many tipis and tipi liners were decorated

A PRAIRIE EARTH LODGE

TO THE EAST of the Great Plains is a region of lakes, lush grasslands, and scattered forests known as the prairies. The lifestyle of the Indians who lived there resembled that of the Indians who lived on the Great Plains except for one major difference: the prairie tribes lived most of the year in permanent villages and were farmers as well as hunters.

The Mandan are typical of these village Indian tribes. They planted maize, or corn, beans, squash, sunflowers, tobacco, and pumpkins. They made pottery, and they had tools for gardening and grinding corn that the nomadic Plains Indians had no use for. But like their neighbors on the plains, the Mandan hunted buffaloes and held a sun dance ceremony, and their men and boys gloried in war.

The Mandan built their villages along the Missouri River. Their houses, called earth lodges, were round and very large, from 40 to 80 feet across. They were built of wood and earth and looked from the outside like igloos made of dirt. The thick earth walls made the earth lodge warm in winter and cool in summer. The roof would be used for drying corn and as a porch for family members to sit on during hot summer evenings.

A lodge was home to as many as thirty or forty people from several related families. The people slept on boxlike rawhide beds on raised platforms that lined the walls. In the floor were many deep pits lined with grass, which were ideal storage bins for shelled corn and other foods. On the right side of the entrance was an altar with a buffalo skull and a storage area for weapons and ceremonial bundles. Some earth lodges had a stall next to the door, where the owner could keep his favorite horses during cold weather.

The inside of a Mandan earth lodge had enough space for several families and their belongings—and even for horses. In the foreground of this picture are wooden saddles. In the center, a family sits around the fireplace. Smoke from the fire escapes—and light enters—through a hole in the roof.

with drawings or designs that reflected the importance of the warrior who lived in the tent. The drawings were often a description of his war deeds and showed him capturing enemy horses or performing bravely in battle.

▶ *Many Plains Indians decorated their tipis. This model of a tipi cover from the Kiowa tribe has a white trail running down the back and around to the door. In the trail are bear tracks and the figure of a bear.*

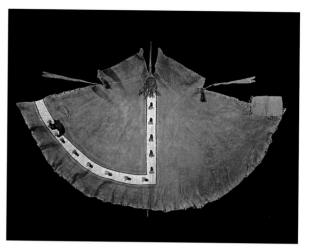

Since there were few trees on the plains, the Sioux were careful to save their tipi poles. When they moved to a new campground, they tied the poles to the neck of their horses and dragged them along. Sometimes the poles were used to make a travois (pronounced "truh-VOY"), which was like a wagon without wheels made by tying two poles together and laying them across the neck and shoulders of a horse. The ends were held together by cross sticks laced with strips of rawhide made from buffalo skin. The family belongings were laid between the poles.

Like their homes, everything the Sioux

▼ *When moving from place to place, the Sioux and other Plains Indians carried their belongings on travois made from tipi poles and dragged by horses.*

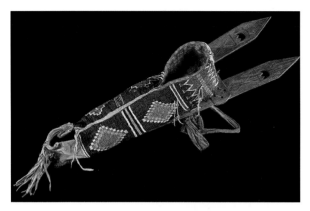

A Kiowa cradle made of buckskin covered with beadwork. Plains Indian women carried their children on their backs using cradles like these.

▲ A Plains Indian toy: a Sioux beaded ball.

◄ A woven water jar belonging to the Crow Indians. Like everything made by the Plains Indians, it is light and easy to carry.

used in their daily life was lightweight and simple. Their clothes and moccasins were made of tanned elk skins or deerskins. Women wore loose leather dresses with lots of fringe, tied at the waist with a belt. Men wore fringed leather shirts and leggings and a "breechclout," which was a strip of leather resembling a long towel that passed between the legs and hung over the belt at both the front and back. In cold weather men and women wrapped themselves in robes made from buffalo skins that were tanned on one side and furred on the other. Buffalo robes also made comfortable and cozy bedding.

Although simple and functional, everything the Sioux and other Plains Indians used was also well made and beautifully decorated. Decorations were of two types:

drawing and quill working. The drawings could be either realistic scenes such as those showing a warrior hunting or fighting, or they could be geometric designs. Quillwork used the quills from porcupines. These were flattened, dyed, and then sewn onto dresses, moccasins, and shirts. Quill working is still done by some North American Indians.

Sioux warriors carried a variety of weapons. Their favorite was the bow and arrow, but they also used lances and clubs with stone heads. For protection from enemy arrows and clubs, warriors carried round shields about 18 inches in diameter. Made from the thickest skin of the buffalo, the shields were as stiff as a board. They were decorated with designs, feathers, and long hair from a horse's tail or mane. The

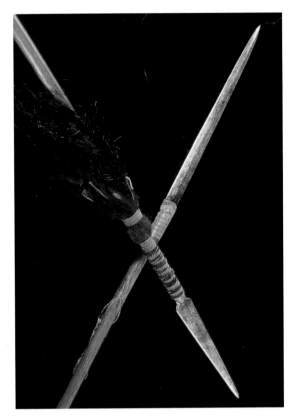

A Sioux warrior's
equipment
(clockwise from above):

A buckskin war shirt.

Steel-pointed lances
decorated with hair and fur.

A stone-headed war club.

Bows and metal-tipped
arrows.

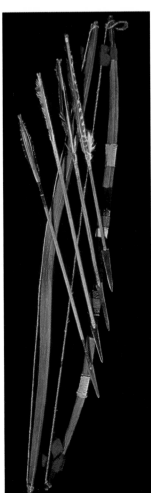

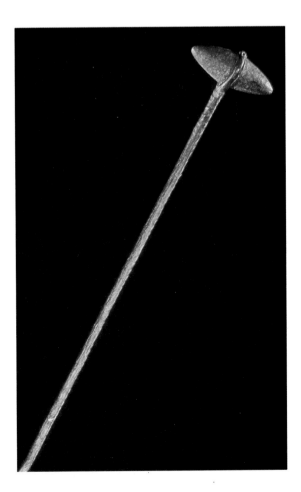

THE CUSTER FIGHT

BY THE BEGINNING of the eighteenth century, Europeans had begun to invade the homelands of the Plains Indians. First came French and British trappers and traders. They were followed by travelers heading west on the Oregon Trail. Then, after the Civil War, came the railroads. Trains made it possible for great numbers of people to move onto the plains. Settlers built houses and cut up the earth for gardens and crops. They put up fences and hunted and scared away the buffalo and other animals that the Indians depended upon.

Beginning in the 1850s, the U.S. government made treaties with the Plains Indians. In exchange for presents, food, and money, the Indians agreed to live on vast tracts of land called reservations.

A drawing by Red Horse, a Sioux warrior who fought at the Battle of the Little Bighorn, shows the U.S. Cavalry under attack by Indian warriors on horseback.

The government, in turn, promised the Indians that they could live undisturbed on these lands forever. At first, the treaties were honored, but most of them were broken as more and more settlers moved west.

The experience of the Sioux and Cheyenne Indians who lived in present-day Montana, Wyoming, and North and South Dakota was typical of that of the Plains Indians in the years after the Civil War. In 1874, gold was discovered in the Black Hills of South Dakota—land that was sacred to the Sioux and protected by treaties. When hundreds of miners and prospectors began arriving in the Black Hills in search of gold, the Sioux and Cheyenne allies went to war.

Instead of evicting the prospectors from the Black Hills, the government chose instead to order all the Sioux and Cheyenne onto smaller reservations. When the Indians refused, the U.S. army sent three columns of soldiers to force them. The result was the famous Battle of the Little Bighorn. On June 25, 1876, the Sioux and Cheyenne under the leadership of Sitting Bull, Crazy Horse, Gall, and others won a tremendous victory over the Seventh Cavalry, commanded by Lieutenant Colonel George Armstrong Custer. More than 200 soldiers, including Custer, were killed that day.

But this victory was followed by many defeats. Before another year had passed, all the Sioux and Cheyenne who had taken part in the Custer fight had either been defeated or slipped undetected onto reservations. A handful of die-hards escaped to Canada with Sitting Bull.

By the end of the 1870s, most of the Plains Indians were living on the reservations they detested and had so long resisted. Where they had once roamed freely across the plains in pursuit of the buffalo, they were now forced to accept a new life they neither wanted nor understood.

designs represented the warrior's "medicine," which was a special spiritual power that protected him from harm.

This spiritual protection was received during a "vision quest," a rite of initiation that required young Indian boys to go without food or water for four days, usually in an isolated place such as a high mountain ledge. The boy would have a vision, which would later be explained to him by a shaman, or priest, and which would reveal his spiritual protector. This could be a grizzly bear, an eagle, or anything else in the natural world the boy could call upon, like a guardian angel, in times of need.

For the Sioux and many other Plains Indians, the most important religious ceremony of the year was the Sun Dance. All the Teton bands came together to reinforce family and kinship ties and assure the tribe that buffalo would be plentiful in the coming year. Young men fasted, prayed, and danced for three days. Many of the men would pierce their back and chest muscles with sharp thorns, which were attached by rawhide lines to a post or a heavy buffalo skull. As they performed the Sun Dance, the thorns would pull through the flesh, leaving scars that were worn as a badge of honor. It was believed that this brought the dancers closer to the spirit world.

◆

The first Europeans met by the Teton Sioux were French fur traders, just about the time the Sioux ventured onto the plains. A proud and independent people, the Sioux were able to roam the plains until well into the nineteenth century, when war with the United States government and the destruction of the buffalo forced them into life on reservations in North and South Dakota. The Sioux today are still a numerous and independent people who value the horse and their warrior tradition.

POWWOW BY MARDELL PLAIN FEATHER

When my parents take me to a powwow, I can't sit still! My mother made me a dancing outfit of moccasins and leggings beaded with flower designs, a pretty beaded deerhide dress, a shawl with sequins on it, beaded braid holders to wrap around my braids, earrings to match, and a silk dress to wear underneath the deerhide. When I dance, I lift my shawl up with my arms and twirl and twirl to the beat of the drums and singing. I can feel the blood in my veins run fast, hear my heart pounding, and the colors and music seem to become a whirling musical rainbow in my mind. I dance until my parents say it's time to go home, usually past midnight. We Crow children get to stay up real late during powwows, which occur only three or four times each year on our reservation.

I was not able to dance at the last powwow because I had sprained my ankle. I love to dance so much that I almost refused to go. I did not want to sit on the sidelines and miss out on all the fun. But as I sat with my mother, she began telling me about powwows and how sacred they are.

When we speak, we always call our dances "powwows," but my mother told me that this is a term that was used by white people to describe any gathering of Indian people. Our Crow word for a dance gathering is *baasaxxbiilua*, which means "making noise." I listened, and the powwow really was "making noise." People laughing and talking, drums beating, and the dancers and singers making *much* noise!

That evening, a little boy who was dancing for the first time was having a "giveaway." This is a ceremony of introduction to the Crow people, showing that this young man would be dancing from now on. He gave away presents: blankets, a symbol of warmth and safety; money to the elders; and pretty material to some of the older women. In return, the people he gave presents to offered him prayers and good wishes in his efforts to be a dancer. Most of the people he gave presents to were his clan relatives, people who belonged to his father's clan. You see, the Crow people have very strong clan relationships, and most activities are not done without clan acknowledgement.

We also saw the young girl who had been selected as the forthcoming Crow Fair Princess be given the right to wear an eagle plume in her hair. Eagles are sacred birds to the Crow people and their feathers are worn in dance outfits with pride. If a girl wants to wear one, she must first ask a Crow warrior to give her the right. Today, our warriors are men who have served in the military. The little princess gave presents for good wishes to a Vietnam War veteran and he, in turn, tied a beautiful, white, fluffy eagle plume to her braid. Now she can wear the eagle plume whenever she dances at a powwow.

Next, I saw a new bride. Her mother-in-law had just given her a new beaded deerhide dress, matching moccasins and leggings, blankets, shawls, pretty silk dresses, and other gifts. Behind her stood a Crier—one of the elders who can speak for the family at any public gathering of the Crow people. In a loud voice, he was praising the bride and her husband's family. My mother told me that this was a way of the bridegroom's family announcing the marriage to the Crow people—just like white people do when they write in newspapers about weddings.

I also saw a young girl given her official Indian name by an elder of the tribe. The elder announced to the people that after praying and considering what name he should give her, he had selected Helpful Woman. Mother said that the elder had been a policeman when he was young and had helped keep the community safe, and this was why he chose the name Helpful Woman. She explained that many prayers and good wishes were behind the name and that the young girl would go through life safely because of the strong meaning behind it. She had a white man's name, too, but among the Crow this is the name she would be known by.

I'm usually too busy dancing and making noise to pay attention to what goes on about me and to how the traditions of my people are being kept alive, but sitting with my mother made me proud. When I have children someday, I am going to ask them to sit still for a little while with me at a powwow so that I can tell them the things my mother told me.

Mardell Plain Feather is a Crow Indian tribal member. She has worked as a National Park Service ranger and historian at the Little Bighorn Battlefield National Monument in Montana and, until her retirement in 1994, at the Fort Smith National Historic Site in Arkansas.

7

THE SUBARCTIC:
AN ATHAPASKAN SKIN WIGWAM

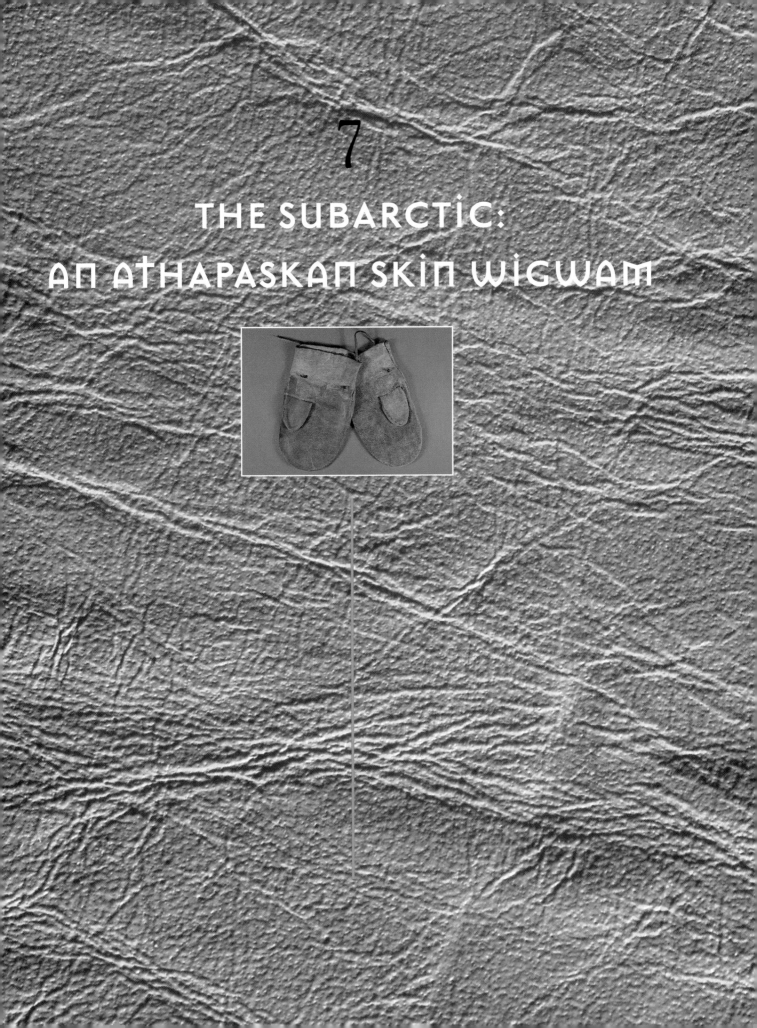

An Athapaskan father has returned to his family with wood for the fire. His snug, dome-shaped wigwam is made of wooden poles tied together at the top and covered with animal skins and pieces of bark. It keeps the family warm even during the worst

winter storms and can easily be taken down when it is time to move camp. Outside the wigwam are the snowshoes that enable the family to travel in deep snow. A second man is removing the body of a caribou from a sled after a hunting trip.

THE SUBARCTIC REGION AND SOME SELECTED TRIBES

KOYUKON

KUTCHIN

YELLOWKNIFE

SLAVE

CHIPEWYAN

BEAVER

NASKAPI

CREE

MONTAGNAIS

THE SUBARCTIC REGION spans the entire North American continent, from the interior of Alaska in the west to the Labrador Peninsula in the east, and from beyond the Arctic Circle in the north almost to the present-day United States in the south. Most of the Subarctic is today part of Canada.

Because the region is so large, the landscape varies a great deal. It has tundra—vast treeless plains that are frozen in winter and so soft and boggy in summer that people can hardly walk on them. But it also has towering mountains, prairies, majestic forests, and numerous swamps, lakes, and rivers. The rivers and lakes are home to many different types of fish, while the prairies, tundra, and forests abound with animals such as caribou, moose, bears, rabbits, beavers, foxes, and wolves. On the swamps, rivers, and lakes live thousands of ducks, swans, and geese. In the summer the forests of the Subarctic also abound with mosquitoes and black flies, which torment people and animals alike.

The people of the Subarctic were known as Athapaskans. This is an Algonquian word that means "strangers." It was used by the Algonquin Indians near the Great Lakes when talking about the people who lived to the north.

The Athapaskan peoples lived in

loosely organized bands with names such as Slave, Yellowknife, and Cree. These bands were larger than those of their Inuit neighbors in the Arctic, but not as large or well organized as the tribes that lived to the south. They were all related to each other in the sense that they all spoke a form of the Athapaskan or, in some cases, Algonquian languages, and they all shared a similar way of life.

Because summers were short and winters harsh, the Athapaskan peoples did not do any farming. They lived entirely by hunting and fishing and gathering berries and certain plants they used for food or medicine. In the northern part of the Subarctic, they were an "edge of the woods" people who sometimes went out to the tundra to hunt caribou and sometimes went into the forests to hunt moose and bear. In the southern part of the Subarctic, they lived very much like the Indians of the Great Plains. To the west some of them lived like the Indians of the Northwest Coast.

Subarctic peoples lived according to

DISEASE

THE WORST ENEMY of the native peoples of the Americas was disease. Having been isolated from the peoples of Europe, Africa, and Asia for more than 10,000 years, the Indians had few infectious diseases such as measles, smallpox, and influenza. As a result, the Indians also did not have an immunity, or natural protection, against these diseases.

When the European explorers arrived, they brought their diseases along with them. The Indians immediately got sick and thousands upon thousands of them died. Scholars disagree on the number of people living in North and South America when Columbus arrived in 1492, but no one disputes the fact that disease decimated Indian populations. It is thought that at least 50 percent and perhaps as many as 90 percent of all the Indians living in North and South America died from exposure to these silent killers within the first hundred years after Europeans arrived.

The European diseases spread rapidly, like rip-ples in a pond after a rock hits the water. They often followed Indian trade routes. In that way, infections reached isolated tribes long before those groups had any direct contact with Europeans.

A documented example took place in 1781. That year, Blackfoot scouts found a small Shoshone village. Because the village seemed unusually quiet, the scouts watched it for some time. No one was walking around, although horses were eating grass among the tipis. Suspicious of a trap, the scouts sneaked into the village and peeked into the tipis. They discovered that all the villagers had died. Excited at their good luck, the scouts helped themselves to clothes, weapons, and other belongings of the dead Shoshones and rushed home with their booty. Unfortunately for the Blackfoot, the Shoshones had died of smallpox and their belongings were infected. As a result, smallpox quickly spread through the Blackfoot villages. As many as two-thirds of the Blackfoot died within a few weeks.

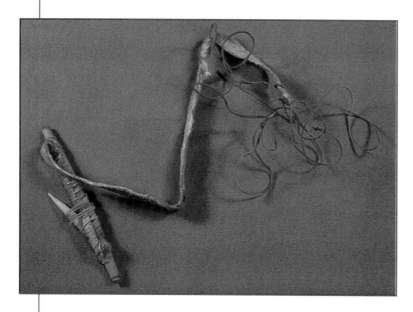

▲ *Montagnais fishing line, with a hook made from wood and bone.*

the seasons of the year. Because they were always searching for the best places to find animals to hunt, fish to catch, and plants to eat, they seldom stayed very long in one place. Changes in the weather or the behavior of the birds and animals they hunted told them when it was time to move. Like many other Native Americans, the Athapaskans called their months "moons" and named them for changes in the natural world around them. February was "the old moon," or late winter. April was the "gray goose moon," which meant the time when the ducks and geese returned from the south. August was the moon "when the young ducks begin to fly." September was the moon "when the king salmon returns." November was the moon "when the rivers begin to freeze." December was the moon "when the moose lose their antlers."

Athapaskan peoples used many kinds of shelters during the year. Some were lean-tos made out of brush. Others were wigwams: domed huts made of willow branches tied together at the top, with caribou skins draped over them. During the winter, the Athapaskans made more durable houses. One looked like the tipi used by the Indians on the Great Plains, but it was covered with bark as well as skins. Poles laid on the outside held the bark and skins in place.

Spring was a time of great activity for Athapaskan peoples. It was a time when the men and women made tools and utensils. Men constructed the frames for birch-bark canoes out of wood from spruce trees. Women and girls sewed birch-bark covers onto the canoes with spruce roots and then covered the seams with hot spruce pitch to make them waterproof. They made watertight baskets from birch bark in the same way.

Muskrat was an important food at this time of year, when the animals were leaving their burrows in search of food. Muskrats were either roasted over fires or boiled in birch-bark containers hung from wooden tripods with hooks made of deer antlers. To boil the water, the women dropped hot rocks from a campfire into the buckets. The nonedible parts of the muskrat did not go to waste. Muskrat fur was used for clothing. The sinews from their long tails were used as thread.

Summer was a pleasant time for everyone. Sometimes many families would camp together along the banks of rivers and lakes. They would have feasts. They would trade things with each other. They would tell stories and share with each other news about their friends in other camps. They would tell each other the best places to hunt or fish.

In the autumn, Athapaskan men began to make and repair their snowshoes, sleds, and toboggans so they would be prepared for winter, which comes early in the Subarctic. Snowshoes were usually long and narrow and made from split pieces of spruce wood. Crosspieces made from wood and strips of rawhide supported the wearer's feet. Sleds and toboggans were made from pieces of wood bound together with rawhide. Although the Athapaskans had dogs, they did not use them to pull sleds. Instead, the women and children pulled the sleds while the men pushed from behind.

In the autumn and winter the Athapaskans hunted caribou and other large animals such as moose and bears,

◀ *A Montagnais basket, made from birch bark.*

▼ *Wooden spoons made by the Cree Indians.*

▶ *A Montagnais comb, made from a porcupine tail.*

which provided them with meat and hides to make clothing and shelters. Hunters wearing snowshoes could chase caribou into deep snow, where the animals would sink. The hunters then shot them with bows and arrows at close range.

Athapaskan hunters also built traps between trees in the forest to snare caribou and moose as they walked between the trees. To kill bears, Athapaskan hunters would seek out dens where the animals were hibernating for the winter.

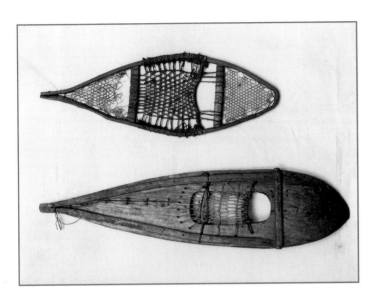

▲ *Snowshoes made by the Cree Indians.*

◄ *A Kutchin hunter wearing snowshoes chases a caribou into deep snow.*

While the men hunted large animals, the women and children would make traps and snares to catch rabbits, birds, and other small animals.

Athapaskan children had little time for play. As soon as they were able, children had to collect firewood or snow to make water. Little boys as young as seven or eight years old began hunting with their fathers and uncles. Because hunting skills were so important to survival, the first animal a boy killed was a cause for celebration. No matter how small it was, the animal was skinned and cooked and all the hunters in the camp ate a small piece. The boy's parents might even hold a feast in his honor so everyone would know their son had become a hunter.

Girls learned to cook, to sew, and to tan animal hides for clothes. Tanning hides was very hard and time-consuming. The hides were first soaked in a solution of water and animal brains. After soaking for a day, the wet hide was hung over a stump and the fur scraped off. Then the hide was hung over a pole to dry. Once dry, the skin was rubbed with a stone scraper and stretched over a log or stump to make it soft. Finally, the skin was hung on a wooden frame over a slow-burning fire. The smoke from the fire would give the skin a rich brown color.

Athapaskan men and women usually had two sets of clothes, one for summer and one for winter. Women's and men's clothes looked very similar. A complete suit included a slip-on shirt or dress with a hood and long sleeves for winter. Pants were tailored with a drawstring around the waist and usually had the moccasins attached. In cold weather men and women wore mittens that were attached to a string that looped around their necks so the mittens would not be lost when they worked bare-handed. For extra warmth the Athapaskan people sometimes wore cloaks made of caribou or knitted rabbit skins. For decoration, Athapaskan women sewed porcupine quills colored with dyes made from berries or bark. In many parts of the Subarctic, people made a red dye from the bark of the alder tree and used it to color not only their snowshoes, sleds, and clothes, but also their hair and skin.

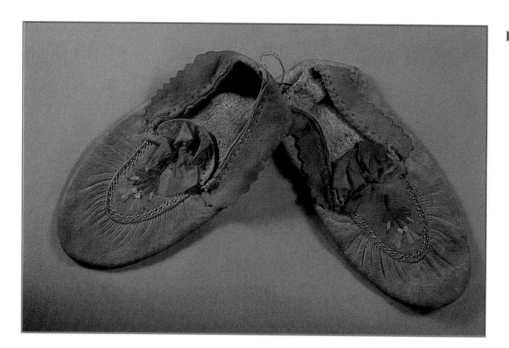

▶Cree hunting shirt.

▲ ▶ Cree moccasins and mittens.

◀ Montagnais children's moccasin.

Because they lived in such remote areas, the native peoples of the Subarctic suffered less loss of population as a result of their encounter with Europeans than their neighbors to the south. Many of them did not meet Europeans until the seventeenth and even the eighteenth centuries. Then many of the Athapaskans worked for the Europeans. They trapped animals and traded their furs for iron tools, guns, and clothes (see page 106). From the Europeans they learned to make log cabins, which many Athapaskans still use for houses.

Athapaskan peoples still live in remote parts of Canada and Alaska and many of them still hunt and fish in order to survive. In many respects, the Subarctic is still a frontier compared to other parts of North America. However, airplanes, television, and mechanized travel continue to have an impact, and the Indians of the Subarctic are rapidly adapting their traditional way of life to modern society.

THE FUR TRADE

THE INDIAN TRIBES that lived in the Subarctic were fortunate because the Europeans who explored and later settled Alaska and Canada were more interested in trade than in taking Indian lands. Only in southern Canada, near the border with the United States, did large numbers of Europeans set up permanent communities and evict the Indians.

The most valuable products to be obtained from this vast area were the fur pelts of animals such as the mink, fox, beaver, and wolverine, which were in great demand in Europe. The Europeans relied upon Indian hunters to trap furs, in exchange for which the Indians received iron tools, cooking utensils, beads, blankets, and other European goods. But the Europeans also brought guns, liquor, and disease.

The first explorer to arrive in eastern Canada was John Cabot,

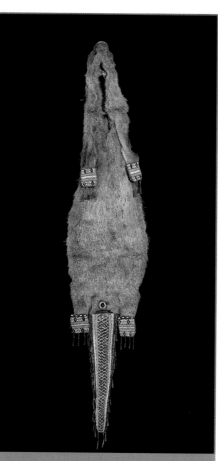

A tobacco pouch made from the fur of an otter by the Sac Indians, who lived near the Great Lakes.

who sailed from England in 1497. He was followed by the Frenchman Jacques Cartier, who sailed up the St. Lawrence River in the 1530s. Fur traders and explorers followed. The French traders, who paddled large canoes laden with trading goods and furs along the many lakes and rivers of the region, came to be known as voyageurs (meaning "voyagers" or "travelers"). The British Hudson's Bay Company, founded in 1670, built a network of trading posts stretching south and west of the shores of Hudson Bay in northern Canada. Meanwhile, European explorers began arriving on the Pacific coast of North America. By 1800, a network of trading posts linked the entire continent from the Atlantic to the Pacific oceans. These trading posts supplied European goods to even the most remote tribes of the Subarctic.

8

THE ARCTIC:
AN INUIT ICE IGLOO

This large snow house, or igloo, is home to more than one Inuit family. Because warm air rises, the warmest air in the igloo is closest to the dome, so the families work, cook, and sleep on a raised platform made of snow. For additional warmth the igloo is lined with animal hides. A seal oil lamp provides heat and is used for drying clothes, melting water,

and cooking. Outside, several smaller igloos have been built to store food, weapons, and other items that need shelter from the harsh Arctic weather. In the background are a sled and dog team, used to travel quickly across the frozen landscape.

THE ARCTIC REGION AND SOME SELECTED BANDS

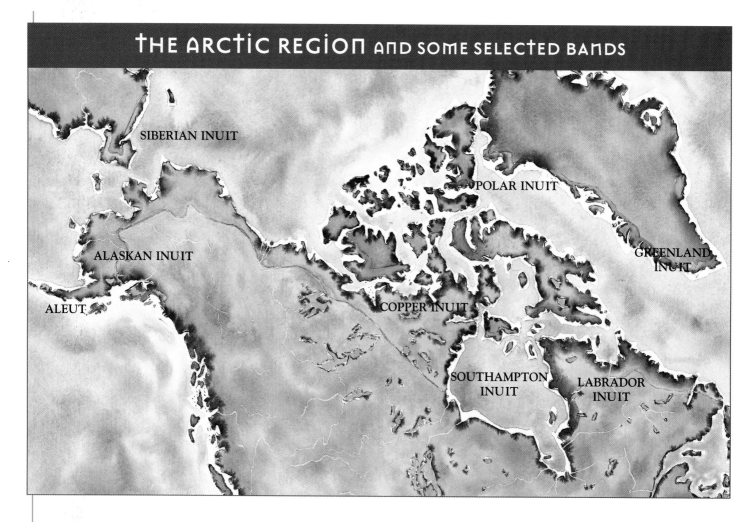

SIBERIAN INUIT

POLAR INUIT

ALASKAN INUIT

GREENLAND INUIT

ALEUT

COPPER INUIT

SOUTHAMPTON INUIT

LABRADOR INUIT

THE ARCTIC IS a vast area of ice and snow that stretches more than 4,000 miles, from the eastern shores of Greenland to the northeast coast of Siberia. In the wintertime it stays dark for months at a time and is so cold that bare skin freezes almost instantly. In the summertime mosquitoes and flies attack both humans and animals alike. There are no trees, only the vast plains of the tundra. There are many rivers and bays in the Arctic, and there is the sea, which surrounds the region. But in the wintertime the water freezes, making it hard for people to get drinking water or to hunt and fish for food.

Very few people lived in the Arctic.

Those who did are known as Eskimos or, as they prefer to call themselves, the Inuit. This means simply "humans" or "people." Because they lived in such a cold, forbidding place, they had few visitors. In fact, some Inuit believed they were the only people in the whole world until they met European explorers less than two hundred years ago.

The Inuit were one of the few groups of peoples native to North America who were never organized into tribes. The largest group was the band. These bands are known by the areas where they lived, such as Siberia, Western Alaska, Labrador, Greenland, and Central Arctic.

indian population, 1492-1900

ALTHOUGH NO ONE knows precisely, it is estimated that forty million people lived in the Americas at the time of Columbus. The largest population was in what is now central Mexico, home of the Aztecs, with between ten and twelve million people. In Peru, where the Incas lived, the total may have been nine million. The population in the United States and Canada was about two million.

The population rapidly declined after Europeans arrived. Most of the decline was caused by the introduction of infectious diseases such as smallpox and measles against which the Indians had no immunity. Other causes were warfare and the destruction of Indian populations by Europeans, and the general collapse of the Indians' way of life caused by the European invasion. In the first decade of the twentieth century, the Indian population of the United States reached its lowest point, about 500,000.

Today there are over two million Indians in the United States. They are one of the nation's fastest-growing minority groups.

Because the harsh environment made it difficult to obtain enough food to feed everyone, Inuit lived in small groups, and few groups lived in any one place for very long. In the Central Arctic, for example, a group of Inuit might consist only of a mother and father and their children, although sometimes larger groups, including grandparents and aunts and uncles and their children, might live together. Because the groups were so small, everyone had to work. Children quickly learned the skills necessary for survival. Girls learned to sew, cook, and preserve foods for eating at a later time. Boys followed their fathers and learned to hunt, take care of dogs, build houses, and make tools.

The winters are long and dark in the Arctic. Because Inuit lived so far north, almost at the top of the world, they did not see the sun from November to February. The summers are just the opposite. Then, the sun shines twenty-four hours a day. This was a time when the Inuit were very busy because they needed to collect as much food as possible to help them live through the winter. Depending on where in the Arctic they lived, some Inuit went out to sea to hunt whales; others hunted caribou, which migrate across the tundra in vast herds. Inuit caught fish, picked berries, and hunted birds. They traveled great distances to collect things they needed in order to survive in their harsh world.

One reason the Inuit were able to endure their brutal environment was because they dressed properly. The women made warm clothes for the family from the skins of the animals the men hunted. A favorite animal was the caribou. Its meat was eaten and its antlers were used for making tools. The skin of the caribou was used to make a coat called a parka. Parkas were large and warm and had hoods to protect the wearer's head and face from the cold and snow. The hoods were usually fringed with wolf fur because it does not freeze easily when it gets wet. Inuit women made the hoods of their parkas large enough to carry their babies in them.

Inuit shoes were called mukluks. They were watertight boots that reached almost to the knees. The soles of the mukluk were made from sealskin that had been chewed to make it soft and flexible. Parkas and mukluks, like everything the Inuit made, were beautifully decorated with different-colored strips of fur, animal tails, feathers, beads made from seeds, or pieces of ivory.

The Inuit also made special goggles to protect their eyes from the glare of the sun on ice and snow. The goggles had narrow

◀ ▶ *Inuit parkas: Right, a special ceremonial "dance parka" from the Copper Inuit of the Central Arctic; and left, a parka made of seal intestine from Alaska.*

▼ *Ice-creeping shoes, from Alaska.*

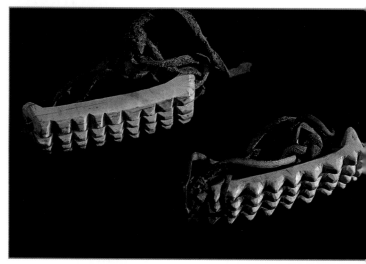

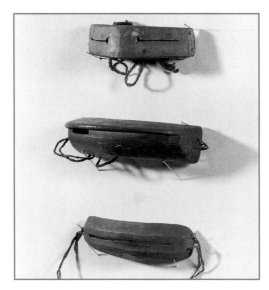

▲ *Inuit goggles.*

▼ *An Inuit hunter waits patiently by a seal hole. By his side on the ice is a long harpoon.*

slits which let only a small amount of light through to the eyes.

Another animal important to the Inuit was the seal. Seal blubber—the layer of fat between the skin and the muscles—was not only good to eat, but its oil was used for making fires and as fuel for lamps to light the Inuits' homes. The seal's skin was used to make clothing. Inuit even used the seal's stomach, which is clear and thin like plastic and could be made into raincoats, bags for carrying water, and floats for hunting seals and whales.

Inuit hunters worked hard to catch

seals. In the winter they had to venture far out on the Arctic ice on sleds pulled by teams of dogs called huskies. The hunters would look for holes in the ice where seals came to the surface to breathe. A hunter often had to wait silently and without moving for many hours for a seal to appear, and then he would have only a few moments to stab it with his harpoon. If he got a seal, he then put it on his sled and took it back to his family.

Some Inuit built small boats made of skin, called kayaks. A kayak was similar to a canoe. It held one or two men and was used for fishing, for finding seals, and for killing caribou when they tried to swim across rivers and lakes. Inuit who lived near the ocean also built large boats called umiaks, which looked like rowboats made out of skin. Inuit used umiaks for hunting walruses, whales, and other large mammals far out at sea. Umiaks could carry many people and supplies.

In the wintertime, Inuit families picked places to put up winter houses, where they remained until the weather became warm again. Some Inuit groups made winter houses of earth, rocks, and driftwood. Others built a special kind of snow house called an igloo. These large igloos could be 10 feet high and 15 feet across. The Inuit of the Central Arctic sometimes made them large enough to hold more than one family. In the summertime, when their winter houses grew soggy and their igloos

began to melt, Inuit lived in tents made of animal skins.

To make igloos, Inuit cut blocks of snow with a special tool called a snow saw made of ivory or animal horn. Igloos were simple to build if the snow conditions were right. Sometimes hunters would make small ones in which to spend the night if they were too far from home. A skilled builder could make a small igloo in a couple of hours.

The Inuit entered their snow houses through long tunnels. Skins were hung at the opening and along the tunnel, like doors, to keep out the cold. Inside the main living chamber the family slept on a platform made of snow. On top of the platform were oars, paddles, tent poles, and other wooden things, covered with branches and moss. Over the wood and branches there was a thick cushion of animal furs. The whole family slept together

▼ *Ivory snow knives with birds' heads decorating their handles.*

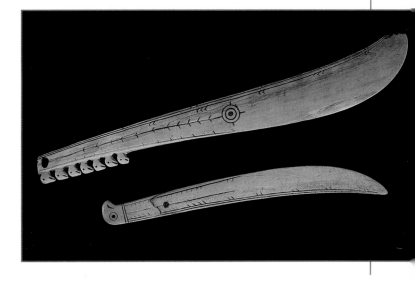

BUILDING AN IGLOO

AN IGLOO BUILDER used snow from a snowbank formed by a single storm so that the blocks would be the same consistency and hold together. The blocks of snow were cut from inside a circle that would form the igloo's walls and were all about the same size—3 to 4 feet long and 6 to 8 inches thick. The first layer of blocks was placed in a circle and cut to form the beginning of a spiral. As new layers of blocks were added, they were tilted inward so as to gradually

An Inuit man photographed building an igloo in northwestern Canada in 1951.

form a dome. The builder stood inside to build the walls. When the last block had been placed, he cut a hole in the wall to let himself out.

After the dome was complete, the joints between the blocks were packed with snow. To complete the house, a low snow passageway was built over the entrance. The builder and his family entered the house by crawling up the passageway on their hands and knees.

beneath a blanket made of several large animal skins sewed together. Before getting in bed the family members took off all of their fur clothes and used them as pillows.

Next to the entrance, igloos also had ledges or benches made of snow. On one of these ledges was the fireplace, consisting of a lamp made of soapstone filled with seal oil. A burning wick made of twisted moss provided light and enough heat to warm the igloo. Over the lamp hung a soapstone kettle that was used for cooking and melt-

ing snow for drinking water. Finally, above the kettle, was a framework of crossed branches on which family members could place wet stockings, mittens, and boots to dry. Some Inuit also hung skins on the walls and ceiling of the igloo to provide extra insulation from the cold. The oil lamp and the skins kept the inside of the igloos warm enough for the Inuit to be comfortable without their parkas, although they usually wore other fur clothes even while inside.

In addition to the main room, igloos usually had several smaller rooms where the family stored food and extra belongings, like their kayaks, that needed protection from the weather. Several families might build their snow houses close together so they could visit each other. Sometimes the igloos were connected by snow tunnels to a much larger snow house that was used as a meeting place. There the families could tell stories, sing, and dance. Inuit very much liked to dance and sing. Their favorite musical instrument was a drum made of animal skin stretched over a wooden hoop.

The Inuit used the long winter months to rest, make new clothes, fix their weapons and hunting tools, and make new ones. Because they had to carry everything and they had little space for storage, Inuit kept very few things that did not serve a purpose. As well as being useful, everything they made was beautiful to look at. Inuit were wonderful carvers. Using bone, soapstone, wood, and ivory taken from walruses, they carved all sorts of objects: statues, amulets, and charms, as well as everyday things such as boxes, eating utensils, fishing floats, knife handles, and arrow points.

Inuit were also good storytellers. They liked long stories because their winters seemed endless and stories helped pass the time. Some storytellers would say: "This story is so long no one has ever heard the end of it." Then the storyteller would keep talking until everyone fell asleep.

Because of their remote homeland and their relatively small population, the native peoples of the Arctic had little contact with Europeans and their lives were

THE ONLY PEOPLE ON EARTH

THE INUIT WERE the most isolated of the Native Americans. Because they lived in small groups in a vast, inhospitable land, they had little contact with outsiders. Some did not encounter Europeans until the nineteenth century, more than three hundred years after Columbus's voyages to the Americas.

One group, known as the Polar Inuit, did not meet Europeans for the first time until 1818, when the Scottish explorer John Ross visited their home in northwestern Greenland. Until that moment, the Polar Inuit—who are the world's northernmost human population—believed they were the only people on Earth.

The Polar Inuit never numbered more than two or three hundred people, and that is still the size of their population. Today they are considered citizens of Denmark.

largely unaffected by the European settlement of the Americas. No one attempted to take away their land or force them to change their way of life.

The Inuit still live in the Arctic. They still hunt and fish for much of their food, but they use modern weapons and snowmobiles. Most live in large communities and have electricity and television and warm houses, but they still love to carve and to tell stories and to dance and sing through the long Arctic winters.

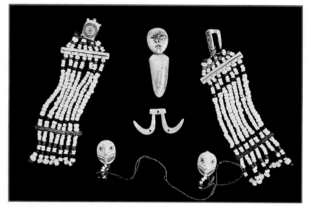

Examples of the many beautifully decorated objects made by the Inuit.

Above: An Inuit wooden dish. On the inside is a painting of a reindeer and a mythical reindeer (on the left, with the strange, treelike back legs and tail) roped together.

Right, from top to bottom:
Three tiny ivory bird carvings from Alaska.

Inuit earrings.

Inuit tobacco boxes.

Inuit mask, representing a puffin.

AFTERWORD

• •

INDIANS LIVING IN TODAY'S WORLD

BY GEORGE P. HORSE CAPTURE

When I was a young Indian child living on the Fort Belknap Indian Reservation in northern Montana, life was good. Several of us lived with our grandmother, as was the custom in those days, and we were happy and innocent. Our days were filled with love, play, curiosity, discovery, animals, and everything else. Our family didn't have an automobile, television, or even a radio, but we didn't need them, and we thought everyone lived in a similar world.

There was no Head Start program or kindergarten to prepare us for school, and when the time came to enter first grade we had to catch a bus in the early morning to a public school, four miles away in the nearest off-reservation town. Bright-eyed and happy, we wanted to go to school, learn about things, and have fun. Full of hope, we met the white men and their children for the first time up close.

But as school progressed, difficulties developed as we found out we were seen as being different from the white townfolk. In town, all the parents had jobs and automobiles, wore new clothes, ate well and often. The books were full of their heroes, from Jesus to Elvis Presley, and they were all white—not one of them came from our world. Everything in this world was white, except us. We became strangers in our own land; it was as if we were mushrooms popping up overnight, with no past and only a short future.

The local non-Indian children made fun of us at every turn, ridiculing us for our straight black hair, our well-worn clothes, the different way we talked and lived.

This ridicule and racism took form and settled in many of our hearts and souls, forever ending our innocence and causing many of us to retreat within ourselves, limiting our potential and causing us to dislike white people. A few of us struggled on and eventually made it through school, because we knew that we were as good or better than anyone else. Reaching adulthood, we had gained some confidence through our successes, and we tried to live as the outsiders, far away from the reservation in the cities. Carrying a briefcase and driving in a fancy car, and buying more things than the people who lived next door, we tried to live like the white people. We found ourselves in a world where money was more important than anything else, and each family lived by themselves, separate from their neighbors.

In the late 1960s, there came a time when the people who were not white began to look at themselves and realized that they should not be considered second-class citizens because of the color of their skins: the contents of their hearts, brains, and souls should be more important. The American Indian people began to search for their traditions and history. Slowly the truth began to emerge. Knowledge sought by studying in libraries and archives revealed many important things.

In the case of our tribe, we found that we had accomplished great historical feats. Our leaders were patriots who fought against the outsiders who invaded our country, and that is always an honorable and noble cause. Others were great medicine men and healers who had a close relationship to the One Above in the heavens. We learned that our people have been in this country well over twelve thousand years, and the way of life that we developed over this long period of time worked best for us. It achieved a natural balance between Mother Earth and her other animals, and the religious beliefs of our people.

Other research produced drawings and photographs of our tribal leaders, so we could finally put faces with the famous names that came to us from our heritage over the years. Our art styles became known to us once again. Some of our language, in its written form, unfolded and became more important to us.

By looking around, many Indian people decided it was better to be Indian than a second-class white person. More and more Indian people returned to the ancient spiritual ways that have been with us since the beginning. These old ways were new to many of us, but we felt good with them because they fit within us better than anything else. They were good for our souls because they were ours: they provided us with renewed energy and hope.

So today, although our beloved buffalo are gone and our lifestyle has changed, the traditional Indian values and ways are returning. People are practicing Indian religion more and more, and are attempting to relearn their native languages. We feel good about this new old way because it is our way. It is our responsibility to never let this loss happen again, for we are not white people, we are Indian people and we are proud of this difference.

Other things haven't changed very much. Most people in this country know very little about us and many believe we are extinct. Schools do not teach much about us; we are only recognized in the movies and television—and then they only tell about long ago when we were buffalo warriors and lived in tipis. Until the true story of our race becomes part of the school curriculum, there will always be ignorance about us, and it will grow and continue to smother both races. People still judge us by our color. State governments, farmers, mining companies, and many others still want our water, mountains, and lands. They do not realize that these actions are making us stronger and drawing us together as a people.

So if you happen to travel to Indian country and enter our reservation, remember you are welcome, no matter what others might say. If you should be so fortunate as to be here during our summer powwows, stop by and visit us. Come and eat with us. Look at our world and meet us—our elders, parents, children, and leaders. For this is when we celebrate our old traditions and you will find us dressed in our festive attire for a brief time. Listen to our songs and even come and dance with us as we celebrate life. It is a good day to be Indian!

George Horse Capture, shown here with author Herman Viola (right), was born on the Fort Belknap Indian Reservation in Montana and is an enrolled Gros Ventre tribal member. He has taught Native American studies at Montana State University and elsewhere, written numerous scholarly and popular articles on Native American history and culture, and served as a consultant to various museums, filmmakers, and tribal organizations.

1492 Christopher Columbus reaches the Americas

	1500			**1600**			
THE SOUTHEAST	**1513-21** Juan Ponce de León (Spain) explores Florida	**1539-43** Hernando De Soto (Spain) explores the Mississippi	**1565** First permanent European settlement in North America founded at St. Augustine (Florida) by Spanish settlers				**1682** René de La Salle claims Louisiana for France
THE SOUTHWEST		**1540-42** Francisco de Coronado (Spain) explores the Southwest		**c.1600** First horses arrive in North America from Mexico	**1609** City of Santa Fe (New Mexico) founded by Spanish	**1680** Pueblo Indian revolt drives Spanish out of New Mexico	**1689** Spain begins reconquest of New Mexico
THE WEST		**1542** Juan Cabrillo (Spain) explores California coast	**1578-79** Francis Drake (England) explores California coast				
THE NORTHEAST		**1534-41** Jacques Cartier (France) explores St. Lawrence River	**c.1570** Iroquois Confederacy founded	**1607** First permanent English settlement founded at Jamestown (Virginia)	**1609-10** Henry Hudson (Holland) explores Hudson River	**1616-20** and **1633-35** Smallpox epidemics among New England Indians	**1689-1763** French and Indian Wars between English and French and their Indian allies
THE NORTHWEST							
THE GREAT PLAINS							
THE SUBARCTIC	**1497** John Cabot (England) explores eastern Canadian coast						**1670** Hudson's Bay Company founded
THE ARCTIC			**1576-78** Martin Frobisher (England) explores Northwest Passage, encounters Inuit				
ESTIMATED INDIAN POPULATION OF NORTH AMERICA	1.9 million			1.8 million			
ESTIMATED EUROPEAN POPULATION OF NORTH AMERICA							

1738
Smallpox epidemic among Cherokee Indians

1813-14
Creek War between U.S. and Creek Indians

1817-18 and **1835-42**
Seminole Wars between U.S. and Seminole Indians

1831-39
Relocation of southeastern tribes to Oklahoma

1780
Smallpox epidemic among Texas and New Mexico Indians

1769
Gaspar de Portolá claims California for Spain. First Spanish mission in California founded at San Diego.

1821
Mexican independence from Spain leading to decline of Catholic missions in North America

1848-49
California Gold Rush

1850
Cholera epidemic among Great Basin Indians

1741
Vitus Bering (Russia) explores Alaska

1774
Juan Pérez (Spain) explores Northwest Coast

1776-78
James Cook (England) explores Northwest Coast

1784
First permanent Russian settlement founded at Kodiak Island (Alaska)

1799
Russian-American trading company founded

1812
Fort Ross (California) built by Russian traders

1837
Smallpox epidemic among Mandan and Hidatsa Indians

1862-64
Sioux uprising in Minnesota and North Dakota

1866-68
Bozeman Trail war between U.S. and Plains Indians

1869
Transcontinental railroad completed

1869-70
Smallpox epidemic among Canadian Plains Indians

1876-77
Black Hills War between U.S. and Plains Indians

1881-86
War between U.S. and Apaches

1885
Last buffalo herd destroyed

1727-43
Sieur de La Vérendrye (France) explores the Great Plains

1746
Typhoid epidemic among Nova Scotia Indians

1789-93
Alexander Mackenzie (Canada) makes first overland crossing of North America

1818
John Ross visits Polar Inuit in Greenland

1902
Typhus epidemic kills Inuit population of Southampton Island

1.4 million		1 million	770,000	530,000
250,000	2 million	5 million	23 million	92 million

GLOSSARY OF NATIVE AMERICAN TRIBES

ABENAKI (ab-uh-NAHK-ee) *Northeast* Lived in present-day Maine in longhouses and wigwams. Hunted game, collected wild plants, and grew corn. Name means "easterners."

ALEUT (uh-LOOT) *Arctic* Lived on the islands of western Alaska in earth-covered houses. Hunted seals, sea lions, otters, and walruses. Closely related to the *Inuit,* their name comes from an *Inuit* word for "island."

ALGONQUIN (al-GON-kwin) *Northeast* Lived in the Ottawa Valley of Ontario and Quebec in wigwams. Used birch-bark canoes, toboggans, and snowshoes for transport, and hunted deer, beaver, caribou, and moose.

APACHE (uh-PATCH-ee) *Southwest* Nomadic tribe related to the *Navajo.* Lived in dome-shaped shelters made of grass and animal hides.

ARAPAHO (uh-RAP-uh-ho) *Great Plains* Buffalo-hunting tribe that lived in Colorado and Wyoming in buffalo-hide tipis. Name means "trader."

BEAVER (BEE-vuhr) *Subarctic* Lived in Alberta and British Columbia along the Peace River in tipis made of caribou and moose hides. Hunted fish, moose, caribou, buffaloes, and beaver.

BELLA BELLA (bel-uh BEL-uh) *Northwest* Lived in British Columbia in cedar plankhouses and fished for salmon and other seafood.

BELLA COOLA (bel-uh KOO-luh) *Northwest* Lived at the mouth of the Bella Coola River in British Columbia in plankhouses. Hunted salmon and other fish.

BLACKFOOT (BLAK-foot) *Great Plains* Tipi-dwelling tribe that lived in Montana and Alberta. Hunted buffaloes and other game. Name comes from their moccasins, which were blackened by the ashes from their campfires.

CADDO (KAD-oh) *Southeast* Lived in Arkansas and Louisiana in large earth lodges and grew corn, beans, and squash. Name means "chief."

CATAWBA (kuh-TAW-buh) *Southeast* Lived in South Carolina in bark houses. Grew corn and squash and hunted game. Name means "people of the river."

CAYUGA (kah-YOO-guh) *Northeast* One of the tribes of the Iroquois Confederacy. Lived in longhouses and hunted game and collected wild plants.

CHEROKEE (CHER-uh-kee) *Southeast* Lived in the region where Georgia, Tennessee, and the Carolinas meet in villages of clay- and mat-covered houses. Grew corn and other foods and hunted game.

CHEYENNE (shy-AN) *Great Plains* Buffalo-hunting tribe that lived on the plains of North Dakota in hide tipis. Name means "people of strange speech."

CHICKASAW (CHIK-uh-saw) *Southeast* Lived in villages of large earth houses in Mississippi and Tennessee. Grew corn, squash, and other foods and hunted game.

CHINOOK (shi-NOOK) *Northwest* Lived in large cedar plankhouses and fished for salmon and other seafood. Noted for their fine carvings and giant cedar canoes.

CHIPEWYAN (chip-uh-WY-uhn) *Subarctic* A numerous tribe that followed caribou herds and lived in caribou-skin wigwams. Name comes from a *Cree* word meaning "pointed skins," after their parkas and shirts, which were decorated with animal tails.

CHIPPEWA *see* OJIBWA

CHOCTAW (CHAHK-taw) *Southeast* Lived in thatched houses in Mississippi and farmed corn and other foods.

CHUMASH (CHOO-mahsh) *West* Lived on the southern California coast and the Channel Islands in houses made of reeds. Fished on the ocean and gathered acorns and other nuts and berries and hunted game.

COMANCHE (kuh-MAN-chee) *Great Plains* Lived in tipis on the plains of western Texas, hunting buffaloes and other game and gathering berries and plants.

CREE (kree) *Subarctic* Lived in birch-bark wigwams and skin tipis and hunted rabbits, moose, bear, and ducks.

CREEK (kreek) *Southeast* Lived in thatched houses along creeks and rivers in Alabama and Georgia, hence their name. Grew corn, squash, and other foods.

CROW (kro) *Great Plains* Tipi-dwelling tribe of Montana and Wyoming. Hunted deer and buffaloes.

DELAWARE (DEL-uh-wear) *Northeast* Lived in round-roofed longhouses in Delaware, New Jersey, and Pennsylvania, farming corn and other foods, and fishing.

ESKIMO *see* INUIT

FOX (fahks) *Northeast* Lived near Lake Winnebago in Wisconsin in large bark-covered wigwams and mat-covered houses. Planted corn, beans, and pumpkins and hunted bear, deer, and other game. Closely related to the *Sac.*

GABRIELINO (gah-bree-uh-LEE-no) *West* Name

comes from the Spanish mission of San Gabriel, built where this tribe lived on the southern California coast in reed houses and fished, hunted, and gathered acorns and other wild foods.

GROS VENTRE (gro VAHNT) *Great Plains*   Buffalo-hunting tribe of the northern Great Plains. Name is French for "big belly."

HAIDA (HY-duh) *Northwest*   Lived in plankhouses on the Queen Charlotte Islands off the coast of British Columbia. Hunted fish and game and gathered wild plants. Name means "the people."

HIDATSA (hee-DAHT-sah) *Great Plains*   Lived in large earth lodges along the Missouri and Knife rivers. Hunted game and grew corn and other foods.

HOPI (HO-pee) *Southwest*   Lived in adobe pueblo houses in Arizona, growing corn and other foods. Name means "peaceful people."

HURON (HYOOR-on) *Northeast*   Lived in longhouses in Ontario. Planted corn, squash, and beans, but depended mainly on trade for their livelihood. Name means "boar-like."

INUIT (IN-oo-it) *Arctic*   Lived in the extreme north of Alaska, Canada, Greenland, and Siberia in ice houses and skin tents. Name means "humans" or "people."

KICKAPOO (KICK-uh-poo) *Northeast*   Lived in Wisconsin in bark wigwams. Grew much of their food, but also hunted game and gathered wild plants.

KIOWA (KY-uh-wuh) *Great Plains*   Lived in tipis in Oklahoma and Texas. Hunted meat and gathered wild plants.

KLAMATH (KLAM-uhth) *West*   Lived in southern Oregon and northern California in large, round earth lodges. Subsisted mainly on water lily roots, supplementing these with fish, meat, and wild plants.

KOYUKON (koi-yoo-KON) *Subarctic*   Lived along the Koyukuk River in Alaska, hunting game, fishing, and gathering wild plants.

KUTCHIN (KOOCH-in) *Subarctic*   A group of tribes that lived along the Yukon River in Alaska in skin-covered tents. Hunted moose and caribou and fished for salmon, pike, and other fish.

KWAKIUTL (kwah-kee-OOT-l) *Northwest*   Lived on Vancouver Island in British Columbia in plankhouses made of cedar trees. Fished, hunted, and gathered wild plants. Name means "beach on the north side of the water."

LAKOTA *see* SIOUX

MAKAH (muh-KAW) *Northwest*   Lived on the coast of Washington State in plankhouses. Hunted whales and halibut.

MANDAN (MAN-dan) *Great Plains*   Lived in earth lodges and tipis in North and South Dakota. Grew corn, hunted meat, and gathered wild foods.

MASSACHUSETT (mas-uh-CHOO-sit) *Northeast*   Lived on Massachusetts Bay. Name means "at the great hills."

MICMAC (MIK-mak) *Northeast*   Lived in Nova Scotia and New Brunswick in conical wigwams. Hunted meat and fished and foraged for wild plants.

MIWOK (MEE-wok) *West*   Lived in northern California in conical shelters and earth lodges. Collected acorns and wild plants, fished, and hunted meat. Name means "man."

MODOC (MO-dahk) *West*   Lived in earth lodges in northern California and southern Oregon, hunting game and gathering wild plants.

MOHAVE (mo-HAH-vee) *Southwest*   Lived along the Colorado River in Arizona and California in flat-roofed houses thatched with arrowweed. Grew corn, beans, squash, and pumpkins. Name means "three mountains."

MOHAWK (MO-hawk) *Northeast*   Lived in longhouses in north central New York State. Primarily farmers of corn, beans, and squash, but also collected wild foods, hunted, and fished. Name means "man eaters."

MONTAGNAIS (mon-tuhn-YAY) *Subarctic*   Lived in Quebec and Labrador in birch-bark wigwams. Hunted moose, caribou, ducks, and geese. Name is a French word for "mountaineers."

NASKAPI (NAS-kuh-pee) *Subarctic*   Lived in eastern Canada in caribou-skin tipis and hunted fox, otter, and other small animals.

NATCHEZ (NATCH-iz) *Southeast*   Lived in Mississippi in rectangular thatched houses. Raised corn in addition to hunting, fishing, and gathering wild plants.

NAVAJO (NAV-uh-ho) *Southwest*   Lived in New Mexico and Arizona in domed houses called hogans. Raised corn, gathered wild plants, and hunted meat. Name means "large field."

NEZ PERCÉ (nez pehr-SAY) *West*   Lived in Idaho, northeastern Oregon, and southeastern Washington in rectangular, A-shaped houses and tipis. Lived on fish, meat, wild plants, and roots. Name means "pierced noses."

NOOTKA (NOOT-kuh) *Northwest*   Lived on Vancouver Island, British Columbia, in plankhouses. Mainly salmon fishermen and whalers, but also hunted and collected wild plants.

OJIBWA (oh-JIB-wah) *Northeast*   Lived in Wisconsin, Minnesota, Michigan, and eastern Canada in bark- or mat-covered wigwams. Gathered wild rice and plants and hunted and fished. Also known as the *Chippewa*.

ONEIDA (oh-NY-duh) *Northeast*   Lived in north central New York in longhouses. Raised corn, beans, and squash and gathered wild plants. Also hunted and fished.

ONONDAGA (ahn-uhn-DAH-guh) *Northeast*   Lived in north central New York in longhouses. Grew corn, hunted meat, and gathered wild plants. Name means "on top of the hill or mountain."

OTO (OH-toe) *Great Plains*   Lived in eastern Nebraska in earth lodges. Grew corn, hunted meat, and gathered wild plants. Name means "lovers" or "lechers."

PAIUTE (PY-oot) *West*   Lived in the Great Basin region of southern Oregon and Nevada in caves, brush shelters, and bark-covered huts. Hunted deer and antelope along with rabbits, squirrels, prairie dogs, and other small animals.

PAWNEE (paw-NEE) *Great Plains*   Lived in Nebraska in earth lodges growing corn, hunting meat, and gathering wild plants. Name means "horn."

PEQUOT (PEE-kwaht) *Northeast*   Lived in central Connecticut in longhouses, growing corn, hunting meat, and gathering wild plants. Name means "destroyers."

PIMA (PEE-muh) *Southwest*   Lived along the Gila River in southern Arizona in domed houses built of thatch and earth. Grew corn, beans, squash, and cotton and were noted for the irrigation ditches they built to water their crops.

POMO (PO-mo) *West*   A group of tribes that lived in northern California. Some lived in bark shelters, others in reed houses. Some fished; others gathered acorns. Noted for their fine baskets.

SAC (sak) *Northeast*   Lived in bark-covered lodges in Michigan and Wisconsin. Men hunted deer, bear, and buffaloes, and women grew pumpkins, beans, squash, and melons and collected maple syrup and wild rice. Closely related to the *Fox*.

SEMINOLE (SEM-uh-nohl) *Southeast*   Lived in the Florida Everglades in thatched-roof houses, growing corn, hunting meat, and gathering wild plants. Name means "separatist" or "runaway."

SENECA (SEN-ih-kuh) *Northeast*   Lived in north central New York in longhouses, growing corn, hunting meat, fishing, and gathering wild plants. Name means "people of the big hill."

SHAWNEE (shaw-NEE) *Northeast*   Lived in Ohio in bark wigwams. Hunted, fished, and farmed. Name means "southerner."

SHOSHONE (sho-SHO-nee) *Great Plains/West* A group of tribes living on the boundary between the Great Plains and the Great Basin regions. To the east

they acquired horses and lived like the Great Plains Indians; to the west they were known as "walkers" (because they did not adopt the horse) or "diggers" (because they collected plant roots).

SIOUX (soo) *Great Plains*   Common name for the *Lakota*. The western Lakota lived in tipis and hunted buffaloes on the Great Plains; the eastern Lakota lived in Minnesota. Name is an *Ojibwa* word meaning "enemy."

SLAVE (slayv) *Subarctic*   Lived near the Slave Lake and Slave River in northwestern Canada in bark wigwams in summer and longhouses in winter. Hunted moose and caribou.

SUSQUEHANNA (sus-kwuh-HAN-uh) *Northeast* Lived in longhouses along the Susquehanna River in New York. Grew corn and other foods and hunted game.

TLINGIT (CLING-git) *Northwest*   Lived in southeastern Alaska in plankhouses, fishing, hunting meat, and gathering wild plants. Name means "people."

TSIMSHIAN (TSIM-she-uhn) *Northwest*   Lived in British Columbia in plankhouses. Fished, hunted, and gathered wild plants.

TUSCARORA (tus-kuh-ROR-uh) *Northeast*   Lived in north central New York in longhouses. Fished, grew corn, hunted meat, and gathered wild plants. Name means "hemp gatherers."

UTE (yoot) *West*   Lived in western Colorado and eastern Utah.

WICHITA (WITCH-i-tah) *Great Plains*   Lived on the southern plains in dome-shaped lodges covered with grass. Covered their bodies and faces with tattoos.

WINNEBAGO (win-uh-BAY-go) *Northeast*   Lived in Wisconsin in bark- or mat-covered wigwams. Hunted, fished, and gathered wild rice and plants. Name means "muddy-water people."

YELLOWKNIFE (YEL-oh-nife) *Subarctic*   Lived in northwestern Canada in skin tents. Hunted caribou.

YUMA (YOO-muh) *Southwest*   Lived along the Gila and Colorado rivers in Arizona. Farmed, hunted, and fished for food.

YUROK (YOO-rahk) *West*   Lived in northwest California in plankhouses. Gathered acorns and fished for salmon. Noted for their redwood canoes, which they traded to other tribes. Name means "downriver."

ZUNI (ZOO-nee) *Southwest*   Built multi-family adobe houses by the mountains of western New Mexico along the Zuni River, where they grew corn, hunted meat, and gathered wild plants.

INDEX

Note: Page numbers in **boldface** refer to illustrations.

WITHDRAWN